TOUCHKILLERS

SECRET ENEMIES #2

By Richard Buchko

For my son Marc – my biggest fan,
and an inspiration.

TOUCHKILLERS

SECRET ENEMIES #2

©2009 Richard Buchko. All rights reserved. No part of this novel may be reproduced in any form without the written permission of the author.

ISBN: 1440406804

EAN-13: 9781440406805

Published by
Calumet History and Hobby
21671 Massie Road
Chassell MI 49916
906-369-0793
historyandhobby@yahoo.com

Of the hundreds of millions of galaxies in the universe, a spiral galaxy is most common. In this type of galaxy, massive groups of stars revolve around a central cluster of stars. Over billions of years these stars form giant arms that trail in orbit around the center, a galactic pinwheel of incredible size.

Occasionally, through the random works of gravity, a group of stars will break away from one of the main arms. These spurs, located in the relatively sparse area of the universe between the main galactic arms, create their own isolated neighborhood. It is inside one of these spurs, part of yet not quite connected to the Milky Way Galaxy, where our solar system lies. This stellar neighborhood, still containing many millions of stars, is isolated - in a galactic sense - from the rest. It won't be a factor for many, many years. It will be generations, in fact, before most people even notice the distinction. But once it is noticeable, and once it becomes important, that isolation will form the cornerstone of human galactic history for centuries to come.

INTRODUCTION

The closing pages of SECRET ENEMIES: BATTLE FOR THE GALACTIC ARM left the Concourse with a promising but uncertain future. The hints were laid that the member worlds would accept a stronger central government, that Forrester and his people were forgiven for their crimes (committed out of necessity, it was admitted by most), and that the power of the galactic arm had shifted toward the human-controlled systems.

Reading SECRET ENEMIES isn't necessary to enjoy TOUCHKILLERS. The events are different, the cast of characters is different (with a few exceptions), and it's a different kind of story.

Science-fiction has changed a lot over the years, and especially in the last three decades. Much rarer today are adventure stories, with colorful characters, crisp dialogue and exciting setting and situations. The genre has become more cerebral in nature – and while I have no quarrel with cerebral, I fear we've lost a little of the magic. It seems as though authors are trying to say *look how sophisticated I am* as much they are entertaining and moving the reader along a path. Science-fiction can be serious in its concept and plots, but still fun to read.

Maybe I am wrong about the state of science-fiction today; my perception is colored by my own likes and limitations, I suppose. Nonetheless, my primary goal is to entertain, to take you on a ride. If along the way we happen to touch on some serious matters, if it gives you reason to stop and think, so much the better.

CHAPTER ONE
CONCOURSE HEADQUARTERS
15:21:01

TO: DIRECTOR CHARLES FORRESTER
CONCOURSE HEADQUARTERS: TERETANIA
15:21:01

FROM: CARSO DENNER
CONCOURSE BASE - VERITH 5

MR. FORRESTER:

Enclosed is the entire report of the encounter between the Starship Taylor and the race they encountered. Proxima Ser will be released from the hospital in approximately three days, and I will have her rendezvous with the ship Teretania at that time.

We remain on alert until further orders.

LT. CARSO DENNER
3855-4396565-339

INCIDENT REPORT
15:19:22 - 15:20:22
Proxima Ser, Special Technician 3
CSS TAYLOR
(Recorded at Verith 5 Central Control)

"We set out on our mission to explore toward the center of the galaxy without difficulty. Everyone was well aware of our orders: We were to proceed past Gorup space, exit the

Orion Spur, which encompasses all of Concourse, Brodian, and Gorup space, and in a direct line toward the galactic center for approximately eight days, which would take us into the middle of the Sagittarius Arm, still only 1/3 of the way into the galaxy.

"Our first couple days were spent in Gorup space, which was uncomfortable even with the Treaty of Teretania to protect us. It was 15:20:01 when we reached what we assumed to be the inside edge of the Gorup Empire and we started the trek across the stellar gap between the galactic arms. During this time we detected no activity or planetary bodies worth making note of. Decker, the pilot, seemed as bit agoraphobic for a while, disconcerted by the relative void, but he settled in after a few hours. We just approached the edge of the Sagittarius Arm when we encountered the buoy.

"We didn't know that it was a buoy at first, of course, but it emitted a radionic pulse which gave us the idea that there was a message behind it. The long range sensors showed it to be metallic, roughly twenty meters square. The pulse didn't match any recognizable patterns, and the buoy didn't offer much else of interest so we recorded the pulse and continued our trek.

We had just set the computers to work on translating the message when we encountered another buoy. Since we were within range of a Class 4 yellow star Captain Mrron ordered a change in course. There was no hard evidence to suggest that the buoy originated from that system, but everyone agreed that it was a logical place to start.

The system shows on the Concourse maps as *Terrion 67-4*. We found that it had four planets, two of which could be habitable by conventional life forms, so we sent robot probes to the surface. The inner planet, number three, wasn't habitable due to high levels of sulfuric acid in the atmosphere. Number four, though, was a wonderful place: temperate, stable atmosphere, and with lush vegetation. Thing was, it had cities. They were big, modern-looking cities -- really not too different from something you would find here on Izar, or on Alleghany. But there were no inhabitants - very little in the way of personal belongings, either. We recorded the whole thing, so I won't waste time on it now, but you'll see that the place was neatly cleaned out, emptied. Computers estimated from the decay and plant reclamation that it had been vacant for about 150 years, maybe a little more. No bodies, no destruction. All clues pointed to evacuation. We checked the samples again, to rule out biological catastrophe, though the visual evidence didn't support a disaster theory. There was nothing to indicate who the inhabitants were, where they might have gone, or why. We began to think of the buoy as some type of warning, but of what we had no idea.

We spent the better part of a day there, but nothing new developed so we resumed course, albeit a bit slower now. Another nearby system, *Gamma 23-22*, had a habitable planet, and we found the same situation, evidence of an abandoned world. Though we noticed small differences, the species was basically the same as what we found -- or didn't find -- on Terrion. About that same time the linguist and the computer managed to translate some of the buoy signal, just a segment really: "NOT CONTACT FOR WE. AFFIRM DEATH FOR YOU". It was a middle of the message, and we couldn't do much with the rest of it. At the time we didn't know whether it was a threat or a warning.

We started in again, back on the original course. We found one more abandoned planet, *Epson 33-4*, but nothing was different than on the others so we didn't make a landing.

I was on the evening watch when the ship came on the screen. Sensors read it as a one- or two-man ship, and the power grid didn't indicate heavy weapons capability. I called for an alert nonetheless, and we went sublight. The other ship approached, then seemed to match our course and speed, holding a steady distance from us. I even increased speed slightly to see what the reaction would be, but it matched our velocity almost exactly.

Suddenly we received a transmission from the ship, the same message as the buoys. We tried scanning for life signs, but we couldn't get anything worthwhile, their ship staying at the very edge our sensor capability. Captain Mrron seemed to get impatient --- I don't want to say anything against him, because we never really served together before, but he always talked about something special coming out of this trip, and he was irritated by the others ship's unwillingness to allow closer contact. He ordered a significant increase in speed. By now everyone was on the bridge --- me, Captain Mrron, Carol Curcu, the other pilot Jance Fromme, the Izarian security agent Wessel, biologist Lister Brose, and the diplomat Klein. No one really knew what to make of the whole situation.

We approached lightspeed and the other ship changed course. Presumably it didn't have hyperlight power and we were gaining on it steadily. It landed on a small planet in a system that is on none of the star maps I have ever seen. Our sensors showed a city close to where the ship seemed to land and after a heated discussion Captain Mrron chose to lead a party down to attempt contact. Some of us were against it -- me, Brose and Wessel were of the opinion that the ship had been trying very hard to keep away from us, not inviting us down, but evading. Mrron was in charge, though, and we took the ship down just after dawn.

What happened next was very quick. Mrron, Klein, and Curcu left the ship. We were in visual contact through small cameras in the uniforms of the landing party - standard practice. But so far everything about the planet checked out as safe.

A group of the aliens saw our party approach, and though they were expressionless -- you can see the recordings -- they couldn't have been happy that we showed up. Mrron stepped forward, extending his hands in the hopes that somehow they would understand the gesture. The first being he reached touched him, just touched him, on the shoulder I think. Mrron screamed, and his life signs disappeared from the board immediately. Others came at Curcu and Klein, reaching out with their hands. The same things happened, screaming and dying. It was intentional; you'll see that on the recordings, they were trying just to touch our men.

Seconds later we had closed the outer hatch to the ship and started the liftoff. The meeting party was dead; we were sure of that or we wouldn't have run off like that. The others didn't want us there, and whether that was some sort of self-defense or an incredibly sly weapon, we weren't instructed or expected to engage in a battle.

Wessel became commander of the ship. He had wanted to join the landing party, being head of security, but Mrron had been bitter about being second-guessed earlier. Wessel decided it was time to return to Concourse space and report. The events with the buoys, the ship's attempt to warn and then evade us, and the deaths of the others --- it changed our mission as far as we were concerned. We had enough information to bring back.

We weren't thinking at the time that we had anything to worry about, even with what happened to the others. We lifted off and headed for Concourse space. We were an hour or two into the return leg when the others started getting ill. They started convulsing and vomiting. Within a few minutes after that all were comatose, and dead about an hour after it all started.

I kept the course for Concourse space, but really just waited for whatever killed them to take me. When another hour had passed and I felt no different I moved their bodies into the secured airlock. I thought I must have a resistance and if I stayed away from them I might not fall to the disease. It only then occurred to me that I should evacuate the air in the ship and replenish it from reserve tanks. Maybe if we had done that at takeoff the others might still be alive. That's about it. When we.... when *I* reached Concourse space I contacted the nearest station. I guess the bodies are in quarantine now, being studied for whatever killed them. Nothing was found on the ship, or in me. It's all pretty strange...."

The door buzzed just as Charles Forrester was finishing the report. He opened the door with his wrist controller, and Merwa Yon stepped in. Yon, Forrester assumed, had just read his copy of the report and wanted to discuss it. Forrester would want to talk, yes, but wished to wait until they each had a chance to form separate opinions about the information. It ensured that more sides of an issue were presented, more options brought to the table.

Charles Forrester had been Director of the Concourse since its inception over 15 years ago. Yon was his third Chief of Intelligence and Security. The first, Ian Taylor, died while saving the great ship Teretania -- and all the Concourse worlds -- from the attack by Hurrd Vandettri and the Brodian-Gorup Hybrids in the now-famous Battle of Teretania. Taylor would have arrived with his own ideas, his own plan of action, and Forester would have had to argue vehemently if he thought Taylor were wrong –

which made Forrester's own opinions more carefully considered. The second had been Driscoll, killed by a Hybrid spy while undercover during the construction of Teretania. Dris wasn't even an intelligence specialist; he had been an engineer before Forrester drafted him for the war and the job. Merwa Yon was chosen from a list of candidates, and while he was not incapable of doing the job, neither was he a natural. He was a good man, a Concourse man. Yon was making progress, but needed to improve quickly, or another person would come a long better suited for the task.

"Charles, did you read it yet?"

"Just finished it. We can wait to go over this, Merwa? I want to read it again. The woman, Proxima Ser, she won't be here for a few days."

Merwa nodded. "Tragic, what happened to those people. And frightening."

"I admit, there are some dangerous possibilities," Forrester replied, "but until we get more information about the buoy message and the report on those who died in the ship I don't want to speculate."

"Fair enough." Yon shuffled nervously. "Actually, I'm here for another reason. I discovered a bug in my office, something a level-eight sweep couldn't detect. I found it accidentally this morning when I was moving some personal items around. Charles, we're supposed to be on full-trust terms with the Teretanians, but *this* -- this is unacceptable."

When the Concourse, a loosely allied group of planets, moved their headquarters to the ship Teretania, there was a great deal of mistrust and fear. Teretania was a massive ship, and home to millions of people who had known nothing of planetary life. Teretania was a full-fledged member of the Concourse, with her own government and laws, and it was a delicate matter of diplomacy to bring the center of Concourse power inside her hull without striking unnecessary fear into the Teretanians. Luckily, Forrester and Teretanian President Garl Zavis had resolved their many differences and were able to work together, bringing an unprecedented era of trust between the Concourse and all the member worlds, including Teretania.

"You think Garl Zavis had something to do with it?" Forrester asked.

"Of course! I'm sure it was that Hybrid bitch assistant of his. If Zavis wants to be confidant to that, and keep it on his staff, fine, but he's got to keep her under control. I don't bug his office, or anyone else in the Teretanian government. Your orders were explicit about that, and I thought we could count on them as well." Yon showed a strange balance between anger and satisfaction, which bothered Forrester. Zavis' chief strategist, personal aide, and lover was Canthay Chine, a Brodian-Gorup Hybrid who had taken the form of a human female. The only surviving Hybrid in the galaxy, her very existence remained known to only a handful of people. To Forrester there was no question of her loyalty. To Yon, there was only the opposite - a bitter hatred and resentment.

Forrester shuffled papers on his desk. "Have you discussed this with Zavis, or with Chine?"

"No. If she's under orders from Zavis to keep tabs on us that takes it to a whole new level - your level - and I thought you would want to know first."

"Good job, Merwa. That was the right call, and I'll have to talk with Zavis and see if we have a problem. Truthfully, I doubt that they are responsible.

If not, we'll have to find out who is behind it. I'll talk to Zavis. I still believe I can trust him. He won't lie to me directly, not with the future of Concourse-Teretanian relations on the line. Let's meet tonight, after the Kenredon ceremony. I hope we'll have more information about the Taylor crew by then as well. Deal?"

Yon appeared relieved. "Deal. I've deactivated the bug anyway, and I'm doing a complete physical check through the offices. Level-eight sweeps didn't detect it, so I can't rely on that. I'll let you know if anything else turns up."

Yon left a few minutes later and Forrester reached for his control panel, punching up Zavis' office with a special code only the two of them knew. He leaned back in his chair and as he awaited a response he considered the new dilemma. It was the support of Zavis and the circumstances of the Battle of Teretania, which had strengthened the Concourse and for the first time allowed it to attract some non-human worlds to join the thirty-seven humanoid members. Three years ago Forrester had used the powers of his office and the newly-rebuilt Teretania to help defeat the Hybrids, a genetically-designed combination of the Brodians and the Gorups, each powerful anti-human interstellar empires. They also had to thwart the plans of the evil genius Vandettri. Thousands had died. The entire Concourse was on the brink of annihilation. For his activities, the risks he took and the laws he broke, Forrester should have been removed from office and imprisoned. Incredibly, the final result became a more unified Concourse with greater central powers, a brilliantly conceived and constructed Teretania which now served as mobile headquarters for the Concourse, and relative peace in the small corner of the galaxy which they knew and understood. So much more remained to discover, and their first attempt at long range exploration had just ended in disaster. Now he would have to walk another internal tightrope concerning the surveillance device Yon found.

Zavis appeared on the screen.

"Garl," Forrester said, "I have a problem. Merwa Yon was just in. He found a level-nine bug in his office. He's an anti-Hybrid to say the least, and he suspects that Canthay placed it there."

Zavis' expression was serious. "Charles, you know that's impossible. We would never bug ---"

"I know that, Garl. I'm sorry, I started that wrong. I put it there. Actually, I placed it there months ago, when Yon first became my Security Chief. It was deactivated a long time ago, but I never had it removed. You recall that we weren't sure about Yon at first, and didn't want to take any chances."

"I see," Zavis quipped, unable to suppress a slight smile at Forrester's discomfort. "Well, what's the plan?"

"I haven't had time to come up with one, yet. I was hoping you would have a suggestion."

"The opportunity to see you without a plan was reason enough to take your call. But I think we can handle this easily enough. I'll have Canthay help launch an investigation with him, to "find" the source of the bug. Maybe we can even come up with a culprit. I'll leave the details to Canthay, but I think we can convince him that we had nothing to do with it, without sending suspicion your way. The only problem might be that level-nine technology is rare.

We have it, you do, but only a few others. Still, we'll find a bad guy."

"Thanks," Forrester returned. "I trust him completely, now, though I wish he had a more tolerant view of Canthay's involvement in our affairs. And I would never think you might be bugging my people, Garl. I'm confident that our secrets are behind us, at least as far as you and I are concerned."

"So am I, Charles, or you know that Concourse HQ would never be here on Teretania. Listen, I got your report on the Taylor deaths. Is there anything new? Anything that could affect our schedule?" Occasionally, when the need was strong enough, The Concourse requested that the massive ship Teretania take a new course, away from whatever trade or cultural mission she was then on. Forrester didn't like to ask too often, because Teretanians remained very protective of their sovereignty, something Forrester didn't want to have to fight against.

"I'm expecting more before the Kenredon membership ceremony tonight. I don't think I'll need to ask you for any new course right now. What happened is puzzling, but we're not looking at anything urgent. I hope. I'll call you later." They both cut off their monitors.

***

That evening the planets of the Kenredon System became the forty-eighth member of the Concourse, and the eleventh non-human inductee. Once the threat from the Hybrids was overcome, the Concourse became open, slowly, to non-human members. Many humans still distrusted alien races, but they had learned long ago that humans were a minority in the galaxy, at least in the known portion. Even to planetary racists the logical alternative to isolating themselves from other races and risking future conflicts was to ally with others as much as possible. The Kenredons were not technologically advanced to the level of most Concourse worlds, which made their acceptance a little bit easier; they were nothing to fear. A tripedal race, what was at one time in their evolution a tail had become a third leg, and they remained amphibious. Because they had little to offer to science and industry they had been largely unnoticed in the wars which had plagued the Concourse through the years. This day, however, the people and their governments were welcomed as equals into an ever-widening circle of friends.

As he stood on the dais with the representatives of the Kenredon governments, Forrester used the time to enjoy his own random thoughts. He knew the ceremony by heart, having presided over it dozens of times, and this gave him a rare opportunity not to pay attention. He had just left his office where he spent more hours looking at his 3D map of the known galaxy. The Milky Way galaxy was a spiral galaxy, with most of the stars concentrated in a half dozen arms rotating around the central cluster of stars. The Concourse and all the known humanoid planets -- and all of the yet-explored galaxy -- lay in a small cluster of stars that billions of years ago had broken away from the main spiral arms. This area was known as the Orion Spur. Three races dominated: The Gorups, who inhabited a large portion of the Spur toward the center of the galaxy; The Brodians, on the outside edge and most of both sides of the spur; and Humans, though much smaller in number than either of the others, occupying an area of space more or less in the center. The remaining races, though many, were each isolated to a planet or two. Situated less than a third of the way from the outer edge of the galaxy, only a fraction of a percentage of the galaxy was known. *The Taylor* had been the first human ship to venture outside the spur, heading toward one of the concentrations of stars nearer the center of the galaxy. Forrester's thoughts split between the results of that mission and the ceremony before him.

The Kenredon people, of a species he thought most resembled erect frogs, had been one of the more difficult systems to get accepted by the Concourse council. Though officially neutral in the Battle of Teretania, some of the Kenredon countries had given supplies to the Hybrid enemies. To many that made them unacceptable, even enemies, but Forrester knew that giving aid to someone who would simply kill you and take it anyway was not uncommon. Beyond that, however, there was a growing concern among the human worlds that with each non-human admission to the alliance, the human majority within the Concourse was weakened. Of the forty-eight members almost a quarter of those were non-human, and still other non-human systems had petitioned for membership. Forrester, and a few others, knew that the Concourse may have to continue to expand to where humans not only lost their great majority but became, like many, the minority. Outside the Sirius Spur and the Brodian-Gorup encounter they had made only one humanoid contact, the ill-fated voyage of *The Taylor*. Humans could be, and probably were, isolated to a small part of the galaxy, and this was likely true of all species. The ability of one group to maintain a majority was slim, perhaps impossible. No matter how it worked out, the more allies they could find, of any species, the less likely they would have to face each other as enemies, and the better prepared they would be if enemies found them.

The Kenredons consisted of four separate countries, and while relations between those countries were not ideal, each saw advantage in becoming a member of the Concourse, the greatest of these being the prohibition of any kind of border conflict or territorial war. Initially they petitioned separately for membership, and would have been the first planet to have more than one member, but the council refused. To allow multiple members from the same planet invited separation of the planets governments, rather than the cooperation which fostered better peace. By recognizing a planet as the smallest external governmental unit, the Concourse hoped to keep all internal governmental operations stable as well, on Kenredon as well as on other planets. So the Kenredons were only allowed one representative to the Concourse Council, though each of the four countries had equal representation in all lesser Concourse matters.

Finally, the speeches by the four Kenredon leaders completed, Forrester stepped to the microphones and spoke to the crowd of thousands which stood in front of him, and to the vid camera which would carry his words across the Concourse. The expressions were unrecognizable among the Kenredons and, he noted, not much more obvious among the Concourse representatives.

"There is very little I can say," he began, "that has not been said by those who preceded me. Each time we welcome another friend into the Concourse we create a more secure future. We will learn about you, and you will learn about us. Understanding leads to appreciation, and prevents alienation.

"Though your people have not chosen to explore far beyond your boundaries, I hope you'll see this day as an opportunity to take part in the future of the Concourse. You will learn that our losses have come from mistrust and separation, and all our victories from cooperation and friendship. Human, Kenredon, the species does not matter. I have a feeling we'll continue to encounter more people, people whose appearance and ways will make us seem much more alike than different. And, with a little luck, they too will become our friends."

His speech continued only a few minutes more. The applause was polite and perhaps enthusiastic. Forrester shook the webbed hands of each of the Kenredon leaders, and of the council member they had chosen, then slipped away at the first opportunity. It wasn't that he was disinterested in the new admission. The thought thrilled him. Unfortunately, other thoughts bothered him far worse than he wanted to admit.

The shuttle back to Teretania seemed long. His small craft, piloted by one of his own men, was flanked by seven X-175 fighters. The chances of attack by some radical faction was remote, particularly out here, far from most Concourse activity, but it was one of the precautions Forrester was willing to allow. He watched Teretania as he approached the massive ship, visible from hundreds of miles away. Three years ago Teretania was decrepit hulk, a ship 230 years old and falling apart, a danger to the millions who called her home. Now she loomed ahead as nothing less than the largest, most powerful, most technologically advanced ship ever built. The outer hulls were *forium* alloys, impervious to all but the energy of an exploding star. The primary propulsion was *gravidrive*, a fuelless mode of transportation which allowed Teretania to cover the entire Concourse, more than 600 light-years, in less than a week. When the Concourse was formed the same trip took over a month. Transparent steel shields allowed an atmosphere on the outer hull, and as they moved closer Forrester could see families picnicking under a star-filled sky. Soon, when the ship began its next journey the people would move inside, the atmosphere would be vacuumed, the transparent dome retracted, and they would be off. He couldn't say the ship had a particular beauty of design about it, since it resembled a conglomeration of asymmetric random parts. But Forrester remembered the old Teretania, and just knowing the strength of this one made it a thing of beauty.

The portion which served as Concourse headquarters, though physically part of the ship, had been designated as Concourse Government Territory. It could be completely sealed off from the rest of the ship if necessary, but that had never been planned or expected. The separation, though more theoretical than actual, allowed Teretania and the central power of the Concourse to each retain their sovereignty.

Forrester's ship rested in the hangar and he stepped onto Concourse property. Here alone in all the universe his word was law. It didn't have the charm of the old Concourse HQ, but it was infinitely more secure. Though he was leader of the forty-eight worlds, excepting the military ships he commanded this was the only place he didn't have to consult committees and endure votes to get anything done. He loved the planets, enjoyed visiting all the worlds, but here, this small fraction of a percentage of the ship, a mere eight cubit kilometers of space, he felt comfortable.

A few minutes later he sat in one of the meeting rooms. Chief Merwa Yon sat next to him, along with Teretanian President Garl Zavis, his aide Canthay Chine, Chief Concourse pilot Henn Dunn, linguist Alphan and Monroc, Forrester's Izarian General. Each had drinks and a few snacks in front of them, but only Monroc bothered to eat.

Forrester opened the meeting. "For the time being this meeting will have to remain a secret, which is why I specifically asked each of you to be here. You are the people who will make the decisions and be responsible for carrying out the tasks, and I know that I don't have to ask each of you to swear your secrecy as you have proven that many times over already, so let's just get to the meat of the matter. Monroc?"

The general was a large man, all muscle. He stood a foot taller than the others, tall even for an Izarian. His hair was the usual pale blond of Izar, which looked almost white, and he seldom smiled. Still, women found him ruggedly handsome, and he was considered a hero on his home planet. He rose, and commanded the computer to project a star map on the wall behind him.

"After the events of *The Taylor* we did some long range but thorough reconnaissance. Beyond the Gorup space is an arc of planetary desolation. That is, there are no inhabitants other than plants and lower animal life, on perfectly habitable planets. The worlds are fine, the ecosystems in good shape, and there is further evidence of past habitation, but no current dominant species."

Merwa Yon broke in. "General Monroc, if you were able to find out this information from long-range scans, couldn't we have done a scan such as this before the voyage of *The Taylor*?" Forrester frowned. Yon was indirectly -- or perhaps not so indirectly -- suggesting that the *Taylor* mission was unnecessary. If his assertions about the scans were true, then he was right, but this meeting was not the time for pointing fingers, and Yon should know this. This was a time for options, for solutions.

"The scans," Monroc continued, "were based on preconceived ideas. We were looking specifically for evidence of past civilizations and recent evacuations. The investigation done prior to the Taylor mission -- and we did a thorough one -- did not provide us with that information because there was no reason to look for it. We had no data on where to look for the planets, and no specific signatures to look for. Without the logs and data from mission to help us look and to indicate what it meant, the information was useless."

"What about the buoys?" Yon added. "Couldn't the scans pick up their message?"

Forrester needed to cut in. "Merwa, your concerns are logical, but they have already been addressed. The buoy signal was far too weak to be picked up except through proximity. I'm sure that was intended, since a species who doesn't want visitors is unlikely to announce their presence to any long-range scans. General Monroc and I have gone over the events and we're both convinced that there was little we could have done to foresee this. We need to move ahead to where we are now."

"Ok, Charles. I'm sorry, General."

Monroc didn't acknowledge the apology. "We have discovered that there appears to be an area of eighteen light years where these conditions exist, extending across the entire scannable Sagittarius Arm." He indicated the concentration of stars which sat between the Concourse area and the central portion of the galaxy. "It could be deeper in some areas, and we don't know what we would find scanning from above or below the galactic plane. We are using the *Taylor* report of the first inhabited planet as our best benchmark. In any case, it appears to be a wall, or maybe a buffer would be a better term, between the Gorup space and what lies beyond. In effect, once you move past the Gorups, you are cut off from the central part of the galaxy."

"Have you been able to confirm," Forrester asked, "that it extends completely across the galactic arm, and the entire galactic plane? It must be 600 lights years from top to bottom."

"Of course the perimeter area which we scanned can be extended indefinitely, and it is by no means a hard boundary, but within the limits of our technology, we can confirm. Even this map is an oversimplification, and we're eliminating stars without planets and most uninhabited systems. In a spiral galaxy such as the Milky Way the concentrations which constitute the spiral arms are not well-defined, as you know. There are systems even in the void between the arms, but in the most general way it appears to begin at the edge of the Sagittarius arm, and we've detected nothing inhabited from the top to bottom of the galactic plane. We're pretty sure that it extends well beyond realistic reach of our ships in any case."

Forrester said, "For the next meeting we'll prepare a 3D map, so we can take a look at how Gorup space lines up with this representation, and any other systems around this area. Alphan and her people have worked on the buoy message. You'll have verbatim copies of it, but maybe she could give us a summary of the contents."

Alphan, blue-skinned female from the small planet Letrone, smiled nervously. She had never been to an important meeting like this before, and while the circumstances were quite serious she was feeling honored, and a bit scared. "Even when we were able to decipher many of the words and phrases we had tremendous problems with the structure and organization of their language. It is very different and immensely more complex than any of the species we've encountered within the Concourse borders and surrounding areas. The message was indeed a warning, and it boils down to the simple statement: *IF YOU CROSS THIS LINE WE WILL KILL YOU.*"

The seven people stared for a moment until Garl Zavis broke the silence. "Were there any hints as to why they would kill all visitors? Obviously they were very prepared and capable of carrying out the threat. But was this directed specifically as us, or was it meant for the Gorups, who occupy most of the area between them and the outer galaxy? The Gorups are right there along that outer border, and must have had some contact with these people in the past."

Monroc offered the answer. "I spoke with the Gorup leaders this morning. They seemed to be cooperative, though I mistrust their willingness to help us too much. But they report that they had contact with this species, which they call the Bryce -- that is the best translation, at least -- over 150 years ago. According to them there was a war, which ended in a stalemate, and each group retreated to their own space. They say there has been no more contact since that time."

Merwa Yon cut in. "Maybe we should ask Ms. Chine if that is true?" Yon's dislike for Chine was known to some and becoming more evident.

Chine, who appeared fully human to those in the room, offered no animosity. "Though I have some genetic link to the Gorup, I know nothing of their history. But from my experience with them I would say that what we're told is only partially true. Assuming a war did occur, I think it is more likely that the Gorups were hurt most severely in the conflict. Though not an inherently violent race, their leaders have shown a tendency toward imperialism. If it took them a century and a half to recover sufficiently from their encounter with the Bryce to turn their attentions away from the galactic interior and move toward the rest of the Orion spur, I think they lost the war."

"They retreated to their own space at the end of the our first encounter with the Gorups, the Gal-Arm war thirteen years ago." Forrester replied. "That war was a stalemate, as history has proven. Isn't it possible that they simply adopt a less aggressive manner when the going gets tough?"

"You mean they turn turtle?"

"Yes, pretty much that."

"True", Yon cut in, "but even though they did retreat, within a dozen years they were again on the offensive. The entire Hybrid story isn't fully known, and maybe it never will be, but there's plenty of evidence to suggest that the original idea was a joint venture of the Gorup and the Brodian leadership, that the Hybrids themselves took control only later on. Now, we could be over analyzing and it could all have been the work of a few charismatic individuals within the higher Gorup and Brodian ranks, but more likely it shows that they wish to expand their empire. And if quick expansion is their aim, why move against the Concourse? Why choose an opponent that recently proved to be a match for your firepower? Why not turn toward the people you battled 150 years ago? They would have to consider their chances better against older foes."

Monroc answered. "Their alliance with the Brodians could account for that. It would make more sense for them to eliminate us first, as they tried to do, since we were sitting there between the two empires."

Yon said, "Yes --- if there was not inevitably going to be a conflict between the Brodians and the Gorups. Remember that initially it was not a Hybrid plot, but an agreement between the Brodians and Gorups which was initiated by one of the two groups. The Gorups -- if this situation can be taken at face value -- completely ignored the Bryce and allied themselves with someone whom they knew would be an eventual enemy, all done to battle another enemy that had just bested them, or at least equaled them. Revenge? It is a possibility, but the Hybrid project was quite an extreme method to use. They sought each other out, or perhaps the Gorups sought out the Brodians. Why?"

Henn Dunn, silent to this point, voiced the answer that all were reaching. "They wanted to move their empire toward the outer arms of the galaxy and were willing to take great risks to do it."

It took only a moment of contemplation for everyone in the room to see the logic of the argument. The Gorups may fear the Bryce enough to leave them alone, and to turn all their imperialistic efforts toward the opposite end of the galaxy.

Chine spoke. "All right. Let's work under that assumption for now. The Gorups wanted to expand, but they were afraid to move against the Bryce because of whatever happened a century and a half ago. After the Unity War proved to be too much for them they decided to try again, but knowing that the Concourse had another enemy, the Brodians, the Gorups decided to ally themselves with the Brodians, figuring that together they could eliminate the Concourse. Eventually one or the other would have pulled a double-cross and they would have to fight each other, but the Gorups still thought that better than fighting the Bryce again. The Brodian motive is even more nebulous, but even if all this is true, the Gorups coexisted with the Bryce for at least 150 years. We should have nothing to fear from the Bryce now, necessarily. They seem to want to be left alone. Does anyone see a problem with that?"

"They killed our crew." Monroc said flatly. "That is a hostile act and must be answered."

"They reacted," Zavis answered, "to an unknown vessel that in their eyes ignored every warning and sign thrown in their direction. To them it may have been pure defense. I don't see where the Concourse has the right, or the need, to do anything at all. Were there any indications from the warning buoys that the ship had anything to fear if it had turned around and respected their space/"

Alphan shook her head. "Nothing that we can tell. It was a purely defensive message in that regard."

"Let's make it clear from the outset," Forrester added, "that we are not planning any overt military action. The credo of the Concourse is that every civilization has the right to dictate its own affairs, and while we may not share the viewpoints and the circumstances might be difficult for us to accept, we cannot violate their privacy. If we do, they have the right to react as they feel necessary. Had we known about them and had a rudimentary understanding of their language we would have been prepared for something like this. *The Taylor* did not have orders to return if they came across such a situation, they were ordered to use their best judgment and investigate. The shortsightedness was on the part of the Concourse. I am solely responsible for the deaths of the *Taylor* crew. The mission was rash and not well thought out."

"If we're not doing anything about the Bryce, then why are we here?" Monroc asked.

"We're not taking overt action, but we do need information. We need to know more about the extent of their space, and what routes we can use to explore beyond, by going around them. For that we need everyone here. Other than scattered systems above or below the galactic plane, we have only two directions available to us, either toward the center of the galaxy into the Sagittarius Arm, or toward the out galaxy into the Perseus Arm. The Perseus Arm is much farther away, and we would either have to venture a long detour outside the galactic plane, or travel through Brodian space. Though we have peace with them for now, I would not feel comfortable about the safety of any Concourse ships inside Brodian space. We could travel parallel to the spiral arms through the relative void but, again, we have the problem of technology and time; they would be unreasonably long-term missions. Our best bet for manned missions is toward the central part of the galaxy. Unfortunately this means dealing with the Bryce and what appears to be extreme xenophobia.

"Henn Dunn is one of our best pilots and trainers, and has the best security clearance in the military short of the General himself. We don't know the extent of the Bryce's tracking systems. I would like General Monroc, Lieutenant Dunn, Alphan, and Merwa Yon to work together on a plan for surveillance of Bryce space, manned and unmanned, one that will not arouse their suspicions or fears. Lt. Dunn, it is not necessary that you take an active part in any manned mission, but if you don't your experience is sorely needed in picking the best people for the job. I'll be looking for a report on my desk in twenty-four hours. Proxima Ser, the survivor from the Taylor mission, will arrive shortly. I'll ask her to join you and provide whatever first-hand information she can."

Garl Zavis took a drink. "Charles, why are Canthay and I here? I appreciate knowing what is going on, but this is clearly not so much a Teretania ship matter as it is an overall Concourse one. Unless you plan to take the ship out of Concourse space, and I don't think you are, our presence here isn't required."

"I wanted more than anything to save time later on, Garl. I may ask you to make small changes in the Teretania schedule, nothing outrageous or extreme, but if reconnaissance of the Bryce necessitates a deviation and I have to ask you for it, you already know the full reasons and I don't have to go far in my explanations if I make what seems to be an unreasonable request."

Canthay Chine looked at Forrester, and gave him a quizzical cock of the eyebrow. "You seem rushed. Why are you in such a hurry? All evidence suggested not only that the Bryce have retreated to their own space, but that they have been there for some time. Surely we're not racing a clock here. The need to communicate with other races beyond the Bryce isn't pressing, and might even be premature given recent history. But when the day comes we can always move around them if needs be."

Forrester looked at Alphan, who frowned. "We're not sure," she said, "because linguistics are so uncertain with this race. But there is a probability of 13.6% that their warning is also a threat. Again, the chances aren't high, but certain portions of their message could be a statement which says that any race violating their space will be killed. Not just the violators, but the entire race responsible for such curious beings."

"The chance of this kind of threat being true is small," Forrester added, "And there's an even smaller chance that they have the capability, the resources to even attempt to carry it out. In light of the trouble we had with the Hybrids, and the fact that our forces aren't fully re-energized, we don't want to take any chances. We could be using a sledge hammer to flatten a fly, but we don't want to let our guard down for a minute. If they don't want to talk with us, have any kind of a relationship with us, fine. We'll make sure, though, that they cannot harm us, and we'll do it now. It may seem like some to paranoia, which is one reason why this meeting is kept secret, but when you look at the last 15 years of Concourse history we've found that many races are our willing friends, other have been reluctant cohabitants, but there have also been enemies. Those enemies have often been very aggressive. We know so little about the Bryce. Until we know more we cannot afford to assume they're not within that 13.6%."

The meeting continued for an hour, after a while the argument of whether or not they should investigate the Bryce dissolved in favor of how it would be accomplished. Mistakes had already been made, they agreed, in sending out the Taylor alone, with no firepower and too aggressive a mission task. The desire to seek beyond their borders of their recent enemies and to eliminate the sense of isolation and siege which had plagued them for so many years, had blinded them to some of the dangers of such a mission. Determined not to repeat those mistakes, yet needing to find out more about the Bryce while not arousing their suspicions or fears, they settled on a reconnaissance flight, a two-man scout vessel containing Henn Dunn and the *Taylor* survivor Proxima Ser. Forrester could order her to the mission, but he didn't plan on it. He would ask, because of her limited contact with them, and because she enjoyed some kind of immunity to whatever killed the others. Dunn remained at risk, since tests didn't reveal what -- if anything -- accounted for Ser's immunity.

Monroc, Alphan, Yon and Dunn remained behind when the meeting broke up. Their work was just beginning. Forrester disappeared down the corridor. Garl Zavis and Canthay Chine entered a transtube pod for the journey back to their offices. Zavis' offices and quarters rested on the far side of the ship and even the tubes, the fastest way to move around on Teretania, still required twenty minutes. A slidewalk would take three times as long, to run the distance would consume hours. The private transport tube closed its doors. They sat side by side in silence as it accelerated. Chine insisted they take the tubes the entire distance, though Zavis, like many leaders, preferred to walk more among his fellow Teretanians. She was right that there still remained a danger to him. Dissatisfaction simmered beneath the surface plates of the ship, those who resented how Zavis took office, and those who hated the Concourse presence.

"Merwa Yon is a menace," Chine said almost in a whisper. "His bigotry and his accusations are detrimental to the Concourse goals and objectives."

"Forrester is concerned about that," Zavis replied. "He will probably make a change when he thinks the time is right. Yon does seems to prefer assigning blame to finding solutions. You two will most likely continue to bump heads, especially if we encounter any more problems with the Brodians or the Gorups." Canthay Chine had been an enemy spy, a member of the Hybrids, a small race of genetically engineered beings which were a combination of the Brodians and the Gorups. After being created to infiltrate the human worlds with their powers of shape-shifting and subtle hypnosis, the Hybrids took over the Gorup and Brodian governments, and launched their own plan to conquer the Concourse. Chine spent so much time in human form during the attack preparations that she became, emotionally, more human than Hybrid, and she turned traitor to the plan. Now, three years after the attack, she stood as the only Hybrid alive, the others succumbing to sterility and unstable medical health.

"It doesn't matter what the situation, Garl. Yon is one of those who will always see me as a Hybrid enemy. My appearance may be human, and there may be only a handful of people who know my true background, but Yon can still use that to cause me, you, and the Concourse a great deal of trouble."

Garl smiled as he watched her speak. He had never seen her in the Hybrid form. She would never allow it. Originally Hybrids could only maintain the human form for a few hours before they had to return to their true state -- large, blue-green beings with lumpy shapeless torso, long trunk-nose and gelatinous legs and tail. Most Hybrids described maintaining human form as an ordeal, and kept it as little as possible. Chine did the opposite, and slowly trained her body to maintain human form for longer periods of time, and in the process she strengthened her body and -- either along with it or because of it -- altered her mind. Now, Zavis knew, she could remain human for most of a day, and he respected her privacy when it was time for her to revert to Hybrid. He thought of her only as Canthay Chine, human female, and hero of the Battle of Teretania. That they had become friends and ultimately lovers was amazing even to him, unbelievable to some of the few who knew the real story. It was not an ideal situation.

Chine broke the momentary silence. "Forrester shouldn't allow him to stay on the job, and it's irresponsible of him not to make the change right away. It's not because of me, but his attitude can hurt progress for many people. Yon's qualifications are no better than ten or twelve others on Concourse territory. Forrester won't gain anything by waiting."

Zavis answered. "I think he is concerned about the appearance of stability. Forrester is an astute judge of the political atmosphere, those parts of it you and I and most people wouldn't even be aware of. He has proven to know when even a good move could have bad results. To replace Yon so soon might cause concern among the council members. Merwa Yon can talk, but there is little to worry about because few people will listen."

"Are you so sure, Garl? Most people aren't aware of what I used to be, but can he be trusted to keep that secret given his level of hatred? What happens to me, you, to all of us if it becomes known on Teretania that your chief aide is in reality the only surviving member of the Hybrid army that killed thousands and attempted to take over their ship, to turn it into their home base of the invasion force? That this person in such a high position was a part of the conspiracy, and a willing part for a long time? What happens then? What would the reaction be? And could you blame them?"

Zavis took her shoulders in his hands and pulled her gently close to him. She didn't resist. "Look, you've been working on maintaining human form for longer and longer periods of time. Before

35

long maybe you can keep it indefinitely. One of the most publicized facts about Hybrids is that they could not keep human form for more than a few hours. People, even if they wondered at first, can see how often you have been in public for hours on end, and they'll dismiss any accusations as lunacy -- that's if anyone gave it a second thought. Only genetic tests would show a difference, and even if they had a legal basis, no one would bother."

"Are you bothered?" she asked. "Not about the politics, but about the differences? We enjoy a wonderful relationship, but there are limitations to me being Hybrid while you are human. Appearance will never change that. I'm already a half-breed. We could never realistically hope to have children. Even if it were possible, what would the result be? Tri-breed? It wouldn't be fair to a child to try. We'll never have that, like you could with another woman, a human woman."

"We have everything else," Zavis said softly as he stroked her long blonde hair. "It's enough. More than enough."

CHAPTER TWO
TERETANIA - CONCOURSE HQ
15:21:04

Though she had landed crippled ships on inhospitable planets, and flown through plasma bursts far too close to unstable stars, Proxima Ser didn't recall feeling as uneasy as she did when her small shuttle approached the giant ship Teretania. Natural wonders, massive and imposing, seemed somehow less threatening despite their dangers, but this hulk, though beautiful and impressive for what it was, couldn't be trusted to act as expected. Ser knew that hundreds of technicians, backed up by a dozen redundancy systems, guided her in to the ship bay, but knowing this didn't ease her mind. Being man-made meant it could malfunction, and she felt infinitesimally small as her ship entered the tunnel, heading toward the portion of the ship that belonged to the Concourse.

She fought in the Battle of Teretania three years earlier, but had never been inside the ship itself. She knew the history, of course -- who didn't? -- about how the decrepit ship, 230 years old and falling apart, was rebuilt by the Teretanians with the help of the Concourse, and was completed just as the Hybrids and the evil scientist Vandettri launched their attack on her. Teretania dwarfed the entire battle that took place outside her hull, as Concourse ships fought a stalemate with the Hybrid fighters. Vandettri held the trump card, though, a weapon which was built directly over a collapsed red dwarf star, and which was seconds away from obliterating Teretania and most of the Concourse military fleet, leaving the worlds open to easy conquest. Ian Taylor, in a way she never did understand, sacrificed himself, destroyed Vandettri and much of the Hybrid fleet, saving the Concourse. Now Teretania, not quite world, not just ship, allowed the central government of the Concourse to occupy a section of the ship, well protected inside the forium hulls.

The Concourse, Ser thought, may have saved the human worlds from the Hybrid threat -- there were those who felt the Concourse caused it too -- but while she enjoyed being part of this experiment in government, she wondered where it would all go. Another non-human world had just joined, and before long maybe human-controlled worlds would become a minority. That worried her. Humans, after all, started the Concourse, and brought these other species in to protect them, but humans should continue to control events, that being the natural order of things.

Her ship docked without difficulty, and she presented her orders to the sergeant who met her at the entrance to Concourse proper. Security was very tight here, though once she passed through this area she would have freedom of movement just like most places. Her record and identity were well known, though, and she was expected, so the process was fast. Her appointment with Forrester remained an hour away, so she window-shopped in the main market square. A hundred tiny stores, from dozens of different worlds, offered thousands of items, many of which she didn't understand the purpose of. Not many people walked the corridors this early in the day - the clock in the square told her that right now it was considered early morning - but nearly one out of five was some non-human species. What they were she had no idea, but either these people got up earlier than most of the humanoids or the aliens had infiltrated Concourse HQ much more than she remembered it.

She reached the Director's office early, but once she identified herself to Forrester's secretary she was sent right in. Charles Forrester sat behind his large desk, studying a calendar which was projected in front of him, about a foot off the surface of the desk itself. He used a small light pen attached to the end of his finger, moving a few items around, until he finally gave an expression of satisfaction. "Computer, remove calendar and disengage."

He stood immediately. "Lt. Ser, I'm sorry to ignore you for a moment. I had to figure out when I could fit in a few things. As the membership of the Concourse grows, the demands of the ambassadors increase. Thank you for coming to see me right away."

Ser stood at attention on the opposite side of the desk. "Please, relax, and sit over here," the man said, indicating some chairs along the left wall, resting under a picture of Ser's home world. Certainly the picture could be changed whenever he wished, so this was for her benefit.

"I've read all the reports," he continued quickly, "so I think I have a pretty good idea of what happened." He accepted her expression of relief wordlessly. "I wanted to thank you, not only for your recent mission, tragic as it was, but also for your patience as the doctors try to understand what it is that protected you from the Bryce."

"I'd like to understand it myself, particularly since I'm going out again. I'm thankful, but I'd be more at ease if I knew what it was that helped me, and if I knew that whatever it was would be with me if we came against them again. I've faced pistolasers, and been bombed from three miles above, but there's something unsettling about an enemy who can kill you just by *being*."

"We're trying not to think of the Bryce as enemies," Forrester answered, "even though its obvious they hold those feelings toward us -- or more exactly, toward anyone who approaches them. And yes, going back out again is unsettling, but I think we can afford you a good measure of safety. You'll be accompanied by a top-notch pilot, and your ship is the best we have. Our guess -- and its only a good guess at this point -- is that the Bryce don't have many offensive weapons. Everything they have shown so far indicates a very defensive posture, dangerous as it might be. Our first trip that way was reckless, and that's my fault. This time we'll go in with our eyes open, and your safety is paramount."

She smiled a nervous smile. "I've read the mission orders, of course. If we can stay undetected, we'll get a good look at them. If we're detected, we'll leave."

"I want you out of there even if you think there's a chance you *could* be detected. It's concern for your safety, but it's also a concern for the relationship they might ultimately have with us. If they're paranoid xenophobes, and that's all, we won't help things be being caught spying on them. If they are more aggressive, we don't want to aggravate them. This mission is necessary, because we need to know -- quickly -- what their strengths and their intentions are. The Concourse has no problem leaving them alone if that's what they want. We can find another way to get to the center of the galaxy. Let's just make sure that's all they want."

The meeting between Forrester and Ser was brief. He really had nothing much to say to her, and no information he specifically needed to hear from her. What he wanted was an impression, a feeling, and he got one - uncertainty. Proxima Ser lacked many of the qualities Forrester would normally like to see in an agent sent on a mission of stealth. She had courage, but none of the succeed-at-all-costs bravado of many undercover military agents. In this case, however, that extra caution was needed, so Forrester was satisfied that she would be up to the job. She seemed a bit anti-alien, a recurring theme these days, but given her battle experience and the recent events, this wasn't too surprising. Besides, he had little choice, since she was the only person who was known to be immune to the effects of the Bryce, and for all he knew could be the only person in the whole galaxy with that ability. She would have to do in any case, and he was just a little more comfortable with the decision.

***

In the earliest days of the Concourse, the council was the only body which spoke for the Concourse as a whole. The representatives from each of the member worlds held the power and as Forrester often complained, half-joking, he had to get a vote on three separate days to have the authority to change his shirt.

A power shift came at the close of the Battle of Teretania. Knowing that the Hybrids and Vandettri planned to attack Teretania as a prelude to a full-scale invasion of the Concourse, Forrester asked the council for the ships and pilots needed to ward off the attack. The council, fearful of a central government which would be too strong, with a military power strong enough to begin a conquest of individual worlds, refused that request and severely limited the size and scope of the Concourse fleet. Forrester set about a plan of deception and manipulation, building a secret fleet which would be used to save the Concourse, and if necessary, overthrow the member worlds to accomplish that goal. In the end the secret fleet was deemed responsible for the victory at Teretania, all the crimes committed by Forrester and his agents were forgiven, and the scope of his powers as Director increased. Only a few people know that while the secret fleet gave them a chance to prolong the battle -- and that in itself was a tremendous accomplishment -- their victory was a mixture of sacrifice and incredible luck. Ian Taylor intercepted the blast which would have annihilated Teretania and half the Concourse fleet, and redirected it toward Vandettri and the Hybrid battle ships. Without that single event Forrester believed the battle would have been ultimately lost, and the Concourse worlds destroyed. But what few people knew was never shared with the masses, and Forrester's role as hero was accepted as a necessary way to broaden the powers of the central government and further protect the member worlds.

Now when the Concourse Council invited Forrester to a meeting it was to offer suggestions, not give orders. Forrester walked into the chambers, noted that most of the representatives were already there, and sat down at his table. His visits here had been less frequent lately, and more enjoyable. Today the subject would be the Taylor expedition, and while he didn't look forward to it, neither did it worry him.

The council chambers resembled a circular auditorium. In an effort to appear as open and exposed as possible, The chambers were constructed in such a way that hundreds could view the proceedings. Most of the time only a handful of people showed up, the council members who made up the first few rows of the room usually outnumbering spectators. Today the onlookers numbered in the hundreds as news of the recent expedition and the possible ramifications worked its way through the Concourse HQ. A hum made up of many individual conversations echoed off the domed ceiling, doubling back on the talkers and causing them to speak even louder. As the room filled it was nearly impossible to hear until the leader's gavel hit the marble table in the center of the room.

Enoi of Alleghany led the Council. Enoi fought Forrester many times; each could claim his victories and bemoan his defeats. Forrester considered Enoi to be short-sighted and focused too much on his home planet's interests to the detriment of the Concourse, but admitted, too, that he was a reasonable man, when the facts were presented the right way. The right way, Forrester mused, occasionally meant great difficulty, coercion, and force. Politics in the Concourse remained that way. They probably wouldn't change much, for a long time. Enoi sounded the gavel and the room went silent. He waited a moment while the final participants and spectators found their seats. Calling the Council to order, he introduced Forrester to polite applause.

Forrester didn't attend all sessions of the council, though he always watched the Vid. Had he always taken part the council might consider him to be power hungry, think him unwilling to allow other branches of the government to conduct their affairs. He came when the situation warranted, and he wanted the council to hear the facts about the Taylor expedition. They listened carefully as he described not only the occurrence, but his reasons for authorizing the mission, and his admission of responsibility. Finally, the questions came.

"Mr. Director," came the uncertain voice of one of the council members, "would our interests be better served by tending to internal matters at the present time? What I mean is, don't we have enough going on within the Concourse without creating incidents elsewhere?" The councilman, representing Berren, had most likely been told what question to ask, been told how to start the ball rolling.

Forrester varied his gaze between the council and the audience. The council wielded some power, to be sure, but it was court of opinion which guided the long term direction of the people. "Without discounting the importance of internal matters, Mr. Councilman," he started, "the Concourse has experienced most of its trials and troubles from outside her borders. We've known no civil wars, only outside invasions. We know so little about the galaxy as a whole. Exploration is the only way to learn what is out there, to know whether we have more potential allies, races waiting to become our friends, or whether we have more Hybrids, more secret enemies looking for an opportunity to take advantage of our ignorance. Certain aspects of the *Taylor* mission were hasty, I grant you, but the primary idea – exploration and knowledge – were valid reasons for this trip, and are valid reasons for more in the future."

Enoi broke in. "Of course, we are all for knowledge and understanding, Mr. Forrester. I doubt that there is a person in this room who doesn't realize that the entire Concourse is predicated on understanding and cooperation with people dissimilar to his own race. I think that the concerns which likely pervades this room," he indicated the audience as well, "is that it is perhaps too soon. The last attack on the Concourse was only a few years ago. Our commercial, military, and social fabric is not completely healed. Given the volatile nature of our neighbors in the past, I think we are merely asking that you exercise considerably more caution in exploring beyond the Concourse."

The council could not tell Forrester what to do. The charter of the member worlds, recently revised, gave the central government, and specifically the office of the Director, control over all practices of the military, which included reconnaissance, intelligence, and exploration. In theory the council could revise the charter, but it would require thirty-six votes from the forty-eight members to change the charter. Forrester had more support than to worry about losing control over anything he now enjoyed, but there would be other issues in the future, other votes he would need, and it didn't pay to become to arrogant.

"Certainly we will alter our approach, particularly when it comes to the Bryce. We've already discussed changing the objectives for long-range exploration, focusing on observation rather than contact."

"So you plan to contact the Bryce again? In spite of the warnings and threats?"

Forrester was surprised. The story of the Taylor expedition which was released gave no reference to the possible overt threat which may have been made by the warning buoy. In fact, the warning buoy had never been mentioned at all. Enoi had contacts, information within the Director's office, and he wasn't afraid to announce it to the council, to Forrester. He could not correct Enoi, point out that the likelihood of a true threat was only 13.6%, without admitting to everyone that the complete story had not been told. Forrester hesitated, though only for a second.

"We ignored the Brodians and the Gorups for a long time. Did leaving them alone make them less hostile toward us? Ladies and gentlemen, the scope of the galaxy is vast. Our technology may be superior to many races, inferior to others. We may have friends, we may have adversaries. We gain nothing by sitting here, waiting for them to come to us."

"Unless," came the comment from another council member, "they want nothing to do with us. Must we force ourselves on them?"

"That's never something we would do. I refuse to accept that the mere fact of trying to make contact is forcing ourselves on another race."

"But they saw it that way," Enoi replied.

"Yes, they did. And don't you wonder why?"

The discussion continued, polite but strained. Forrester had asked to address the council, before they could invite him. The interplay, the political maneuvering which had briefly ended after the last war, had begun again in earnest. When it was over

Forrester walked away knowing that the council – some of the council – wanted the explorations stopped. The council walked away knowing that Forrester would likely continue them.

When he returned to his quarters, Forrester made a fresh bowl of *braqqa*, a local dish that Garl Zavis introduced him to while they ironed out their many differences. He enjoyed the dinner, while he considered the issues which faced him, all of them. Could the council be right? Was it unnecessary or premature to look beyond the Orion spur, to seek out more races? Public opinion was split, and while he seldom used that in his determination of what was right, sometimes it made him examine his motives, the wisdom of his choices. In truth, most of the larger and more powerful groups they had come across had been unfriendly, even hostile. The Brodians, the Gorups, each of these had empires larger than the Concourse. The Bryce, it would appear, influenced or controlled a larger area even than the others. Was animosity a necessary part of intragalactic politics? Would they be fighting or hiding for the foreseeable future? But, if they did not seek out friends, wouldn't they simply be waiting for the enemies to arrive, with allies, perhaps, of their own? How could sticking their head in the sand be a logical solution?

CHAPTER THREE
TERETANIA - CONCOURSE HQ
15:21:05

In the Concourse there is only one place where families can picnic on the outer hull of a spaceship, lay a blanket out over a smooth hull, play catch or simply look up at the stars, stars which have changed since the last picnic some thirty or forty light years away. *Hulling*, as it came to be known, quickly became one of the most popular pastimes on Teretania - once the people came to trust that they would be perfectly safe standing on the outer skin of the ship.

Caroline Heskov chased a small red ball across the surface, barely gaining on it until an artificial gust of wind slowed it down for her. She knew nothing of the technology which enclosed portions of the vessel in a transparent dome, filled it with breathable air, created nature-like conditions of breeze, temperature changes, and occasionally even light rain. When her parents called her she would go back inside, unaware that the air was then vacuumed into the ship, the dome retracted, and the ship then propelled to a new destination, under a completely new group of stars.

Just as she caught up to the ball it bounced off a leg, and she stumbled trying not to do the same. A strong arm caught her before she could fall, and lifted her to her feet.

"Careful, there, young lady," the man said. "Those balls can roll for a long way here. Don't lose sight of your mother and father."

She looked up and saw the smile of the man, though something about him still made her nervous. She was only eight, but knew he was out of place here.

She grabbed her ball and ran – not too quickly, so he wouldn't be offended – back to her blanket.

"I thought you wanted to be unseen," said another man standing next to him. He was tall, thin, wearing a purple suit that seemed just a little too short for his legs. His white beard contrasted sharply with the jet black hair, as was the fashion of the day.

"I don't care if I am seen, Cahill," Merwa Yon replied. "I just don't want to be heard, and there's no way I can be heard out here. How many people are out here? A thousand, over nearly three square miles? If there's one place that no one would think of placing a bug, this is it. The technology of listening is always just a step ahead of the technology to detect the devices, and maybe it'll always be that way. I don't want that Hybrid bitch to know what we're doing – not now, not ever." The little girl was right. Yon was out of place, his sour face the only one in a sea of smiles. His brown one-piece outfit, a bit old fashioned, blended in well, he thought.

"I thought she was trying to find out who was bugging your office, Yon. Doesn't make sense that she would help you if she was the person responsible."

"Makes perfect sense, Cahill. Perfect sense. I ran the prisons when we beat the Hybrids, ran them for almost a year. I saw more devious plots, more murders among their people, more betrayal and vile conduct than most of you will see in a lifetime. I saw one Hybrid kill thirteen others, and dismember the bodies in such a way that we thought for a long time there were actually fourteen victims. He wasn't missed for two full days, and almost got out of the encampment. Genetically, these creatures are without ethics or morals. There might only be one left, but she can't be trusted any more than the others could."

The two men walked slowly across the smooth metal hull, their voices low in spite of their own assurances that nothing would be noticed or overheard. "I don't know her," Cahill said, "but didn't you say that she turned on the Hybrids, and helped the Concourse win the battle?"

"It suited her at the time," Yon snapped back. "She changed loyalties when she found herself in danger, and she'll do it again if we let her. That's where you come in." The other man, Cahill, owned a number of vid and Comm-News stations. "It's true that very few people know she's a Hybrid, and even fewer people really believe it. I don't want to attack her directly – that would be too easy to defend. If I came out and said 'Chine is a Hybrid' the place would be flooded with denials and evidence to prove it wasn't true. Zavis and Forrester are friends, and they would work together to refute it. I need something more subtle: rumor, something evil and yet improvable, will do for me what needs to be done. Untraceable, untrackable."

"What do you have in mind?"

"That's your job, Cahill. You have the power to control what sees the front of the screen, so you find something that implicates Chine, indirectly at first, but ultimately causing a groundswell of suspicion and distrust that even Zavis and Forrester can't stop."

The two men reached the exit, a doorway jutting out from the side of the ship. Since the dome was in place the door opened freely. They stopped, finishing their conversation before stepping inside. "That's a tall order, Yon. I'll need some time."

"You can have some time, but not too much. And I've already transferred the Units to your Concourse account. How you transfer it to a Teretania bank is your problem."

"Okay, Yon. We're understood. One more thing. I'll do my best, but what if this doesn't work? Your reasons are your own, and I really don't give a damn about Concourse matters. What if you can't create the groundswell you are looking for. Like you said, all I can do is create inference and innuendo. I can't accuse without being forced to prove, and as far as I know the proof of her Hybrid nature is protected beyond anything you can find out, or you wouldn't need me. What happens if you can't get her out?"

"She dies," he said, opening the door. No more words were spoken.

Shortly after the door closed behind them a voice echoed across the park:

THE PARK IS CLOSING IN TEN MINUTES. PLEASE PROCEED TO THE EXITS. PLEASE TAKE ALL ITEMS WITH YOU OR THEY WILL BE LOST WHEN THE DOME IS RETRACTED.

The announcement of the closing of the park was always met with a brisk run to the exits, as if anyone not hurrying would be allowed to float away into the cold of space or would be sucked into the air chambers. No such occurrence was possible, of course, but a certain uneasiness gripped ship-born people when they contemplated being exposed to vast and empty space.

51

***

Though Teretania contained as much surface as the inhabited lands of some Concourse worlds, and her population rivaled that of most of them, something about an enclosed world created a stronger feeling of community, a stronger pride in being Teretanian. It also fostered a greater awareness of public issues, given that just about anything which happened on the ship affected to some degree everyone else. So when the news started hinting that a Hybrid had survived the Battle of Teretania, and that the Hybrid was currently being hidden on the ship, eyes turned to the Concourse. Even those Teretanians who welcomed the Concourse did so with a certain level of mistrust. Many others welcomed any opportunity to criticize the central government. Merwa Yon watched the vid from his office, his grin unmistakable. The Hybrid, of course, wasn't part of the Concourse government, but part of the Teretanian government itself, though that didn't matter. The tension it created between Teretania and Forrester would be enough to slowly and painfully expose Chine for what she was. And Yon realized he wanted to do it slowly, not so much expose her as to eventually make her expose herself, show her true colors like so many of the other Hybrids did when backed into a corner. This was where his time in charge of the Hybrid prisons would really work. He believed he knew their minds better than anyone alive – even this, the last Hybrid mind.

The comm panel sounded. Forrester on the other end, he assumed, looking to discuss strategy, to find a way to minimize or eliminate the dangers from the rumors. Yon answered, and in a moment was on his way to Forrester's office, secure in knowing that he could not only protect the Concourse from too much damage, but at the same time inflict just enough on the Hybrid to eliminate her, first as a threat to Concourse security, then completely.

He arrived at Forrester's office, walking past his secretary Haz without a word. He didn't like Haz. Too quiet. He strolled into Forrester's office, confident. He reminded himself to look worried. It worked.

"You look apprehensive Merwa," Forrester said. "Is there something wrong?"

"Have you been watching the Teretania vid?" Merwa said.

"I've seen a little of it. Hard to know what this was all about, but I don't see any reason to be concerned. Of all the places they could find evidence of a Hybrid, the Concourse HQ isn't one of them. Besides, I didn't think you cared all that much for Canthay Chine. She's the only person who might be a little worried, and I don't see much reason for that."

Merwa sat, placed his hand on his chin in mock thought. "She may be the only Hybrid left, but it's the Concourse's complicity in the matter that worries me. I'm supposed to be worried about these things, you know. If the truth about her comes out, there will be no way to prevent you, me, and the whole Concourse executive branch from taking the brunt of the backlash."

"It's unlikely," Forrester said, tossing a short stack of papers across the desk to the other man, "that much will come of it. There were Hybrid sightings all over Teretania for months after the battle. Before long these will be dismissed as the same thing. And as long as the attention is focused on us, there is no chance of anyone suspecting someone in the Teretanian government. I brought you here to fill you in on our latest probe."

The comment caught Merwa Yon sincerely by surprise. "Probe?"

"Yes. I should have told you before the fact, but it's really nothing more than a small automated probe we've sent toward the galactic center. It's virtually undetectable by long-range sensors, but we're hopeful it will give us a lot of information about what lies closer to the galactic center."

"You mean the Bryce." Yon sensed apprehension in Forrester.

"The Bryce are a great unknown right now. Naturally, as the probe moves past we will get some information, coded, on the Bryce. The probe is taking an indirect course, actually bisecting the known Bryce space from a trajectory that could not be traced back to our space. We don't want to worry them unnecessarily, but we do want to know a little more about what they do, how big their sphere of influence is, how strong their technology is. We have that right."

Forrester stood from the desk, walked across his small office and poured a drink from a container kept on the cooling plate. He had just defended his action to his Chief of Security and Intelligence; it was a situation that made him uncomfortable. That he felt the need to defend himself to a subordinate, someone loyal to him and sworn to follow his orders, concerned Forrester, weakened his confidence that he was making the right decision. That he was doing it after the fact, telling his Intelligence Chief of something that the man had every right and responsibility to be involved in, complicated the situation.

"I didn't tell you, Merwa, because if it backfires I don't want you caught in the crossfire. The council is not happy with contact outside our space right now, and I was more comfortable with the responsibility on my shoulders, not yours." This was a lie. He didn't involve Yon because he didn't want the voice of dissenting opinion to enter into the equation, and while Merwa Yon was adept at saying what Forrester wanted to hear, he sensed that this time it would have been a little different. "Now that the die is cast, there's no danger to you to know the story. The specifications and everything you want to know is in the file."

Yon sensed the weakness in Forrester. Uncharacteristic. Could the Hybrid issue be affecting him? Was he that unsure about the next step concerning the Bryce? "Are you still sending out the reconnaissance mission? I've been in contact with the pilot Dunn and Proxima Ser. They're prepared to leave in two days."

"Nothing has changed with them. Their mission remains secret, and their orders are narrowly defined. I don't want them to come in contact with the Bryce."

"If you've sent the probe – which seems to be a good idea, and probably enough under the circumstances – why send them at all? Why take the risk?"

"Because probes cannot evaluate," he said sternly. "They can record and transmit limited data. I need someone to be able to interpret from close up. I don't want them be seen, but I want to find out something about why these people are so xenophobic. If they can visit some of these evacuated planets, maybe there is an answer to the mystery. The probe will never come within a million miles of these planets. For that, we need people."

Forrester thought back to decades past, when everyone looked to the future of robotics and predicted that before long robots would be performing most of the exploratory functions now undertaken by man. Advanced robots, perhaps even looking something like man, would accept the danger and be the advance guard, allowing man to flourish in other ways. How wrong those predictions were! The more man spread out into the galaxy, the less he was able to rely on machinery and the more he had to tackle with his own five senses. In fact, Forrester mused briefly, most predictions for the future he had ever read were wrong: from hundreds of years ago when Edgar Allen Poe envisioned a future where man's fastest travel would be by massive balloon, where the individual would practically disappear under the weigh of an impersonal *Humanity*; Jules Verne's vision of a corporate world, where all the technology of man's mind went to making his life one of greater leisure; The prophecies of Halet of Izar, who believed that by this day there would be one homogenous humanoid race and planetary governments would be obsolete. The problem with predicting the future, Forrester thought, was that you could never have all the facts. No matter how deeply you researched, no matter how hard you thought and how logical your reasoning, there would be an unknown factor with the ability to change the future – and the unknown always did.

CHAPTER FOUR
DEEP SPACE – NEAR BRYCE TERRITORY
15:21:07

Most people call it The Void. Pilots navigating a ship through that area will tell you it is anything but empty. The galaxy, though spiral in nature, with arms that trail slowly across the universe, is not so easy to define. There is no real beginning to the spiral arms, no distinct end. The density of the suns and their planetary systems merely changes, and unless you are able to stand back and look at it from hundreds of light years away, the changes are slow and nearly imperceptible.

Henn Dunn had logged, he believed, more star miles than anyone in the Concourse, yet he had never before been this far from home. He looked at the starfield ahead, and while it appeared packed with stars, so dense that he had to squint to avoid hurting his eyes, that was the illusion created by looking toward the center of the galaxy. For the next day, as they traveled between the Orion Spur and the Sagittarius Arm of the Milky Way, the stars were hundreds of times farther apart than he was accustomed to. It was as close to empty as one could find within the galaxy. Intergalactic space, he thought – now that would be something to experience! He trained the view cameras above the galactic plane, and watched a screen that was almost pitch black, only a few far-away stars dotting the image. Beyond those stars, he thought, was next to nothing. Oh, there were comets, particles of matter, perhaps some spatial bodies or anomalies that humanity had never seen. But….mostly empty.

He shut off the screen, not even admitting to himself that he was bothered by the concept.

Proxima Ser slept behind him. Their craft, designed really for just one traveler, was pressed into service because of its speed (fast), size (small), and maneuverability (very). The technology didn't exist yet to disguise a ship, so they'd taken every precaution not to be noticeable. As a result, there was one bed, one shower, one chair, and a long way to travel. They'd left Concourse space just a few days ago, but already their close quarters and lack of privacy was creating tension. Logically Dunn knew that she was doing nothing to irritate him; that even if she was, certainly his habits were bothering her, but logic sometimes doesn't apply. Emotionally, he was getting angry. Her breathing was too loud, her showers too long, her conversation boring. How would he be able to stand this trip?

It was the importance of the trip, he reminded himself, which made it not only possible, but imperative that Proxima Ser be protected. If there was something unique about her, something other than dumb luck which protected her from the death offered by contact with the Bryce, she had to be protected from befalling some other disaster. He wondered if she should have been risked on this trip at all.

Proxima Ser wasn't asleep. How could she sleep with Dunn making all those irritating noises? They were only a few days into this mission, and she felt that worrying about the danger from the Bryce was becoming secondary to the tension within the ship. And that, she knew, made the danger from the Bryce all the greater. Forrester had given her some information, but like most politicians he only said what he wanted to, not everything that was needed. Luckily Merwa Yon took Ser into his confidence. The Concourse, he said, was in danger of being overrun by aliens, and Forrester was letting it happen. From what she saw on Concourse HQ it was certainly true. The Concourse was a human government, or at least it used to be. The true nature of the mission, as described by Merwa Yon, wasn't just to gather information about where the Bryce were hiding, and about their technology. Yon needed to know what caused the *Bryce Effect*, as he called it. Whatever they had, he said, it was an effective weapon, one which needed to be understood and adopted by the human worlds. The day would come, he said, when we would need to defend ourselves against the non-human worlds. Nothing against the aliens, she thought, but really, why couldn't they just stay out of our business? Yon said it was because they recognized the natural superiority of humans, and wanted to give themselves the illusions of being at our level. One day, he said, they would decide they were equal, or even better, and that day we would need to know the power of the Bryce Effect, and make sure that we humans, like the Bryce, were immune. She had the authority, if she decided it was beneficial, to contact the Bryce. Dunn, he said, was expendable. Ser would report only to him.

It sounded wrong in some ways, against her training and her oath as an officer in the Concourse Defense Force. But Merwa Yon was her commander too, and if there was a problem with Forrester's true loyalties.....

Dunn was not involved in their plans, yet. If the time became necessary to bring him on board, and he refused, Proxima Ser was to take whatever steps were necessary. She tried not to think too much about that. Instead she tried to sleep, despite his infernal noise-making.

***

For two days the ship traveled on the outskirts of Bryce territory, the abandoned systems. They made long-range scans of the planets which seemed habitable yet remained uninhabited, but avoided staying too long in one place. Finally they decided that before moving deeper into Bryce territory they should set down on one of the planets and gather more information about the evacuation that had taken place long ago. The theory, agreed by most of the small group who knew about the Bryce, was that the Bryce chose to move deeper toward the center of the galaxy, to create a buffer zone between their space and Gorup space. But it begged the question, what about their other borders? Did they create a buffer zone on all frontiers? How big must their territory be, that they could afford to let beautiful, productive planets sit idle? Of course, the planets didn't suffer. In the absence of humanoid life the ecosystems of most planets could only improve.

The small craft headed toward the surface of 56MHG7 - Proxima Ser called it *Moohg*. A large city stood along the shore of one of the continents, and they chose that spot to make their close study. The danger was almost nonexistent. The planet was on the farthest reaches of Bryce space, and all indications were that it hadn't been visited by anyone in a long time. With that fact, the large size of the planet, the very small size of the ship, and their distance from the Bryce-inhabited planets, they felt certain they wouldn't be detected. They set down in the middle of town, and made immediate plans to disembark.

Henn Dunn stood at the controls and looked out at the decaying landscape. Tall buildings stretched toward the sky, but most had their top stories eroded by the wind or removed by some force of nature. Closer to the ground vegetation climbed the structures, slowly over the months and years reaching toward the top, trying to once more regain the uppermost position on the planet. Undoubtedly the vegetation would eventually win.

"Are you going to get suited?" Proxima Ser called from near the airlock. She was already in her spacesuit, with only her head exposed. Though she had survived the first Bryce encounter, and the first mission hadn't encountered trouble on the abandoned worlds, they wouldn't take chances. The nature of the Bryce Effect was unknown. Terribly unknown.

They walked silently down the streets, taking readings with their scanners. After a while Ser said, "Y'know - I don't think radio silence is really necessary." Neither had been consciously maintaining silence, of course, but the relative quiet around them, the city waiting for humanoid movement, caused them to feel awkward talking.

"I guess I feel as though someone or something could pop out of the shadows at any moment," he replied.

"The only things moving around here for a long time have been these squirrel-like creatures," she added, indicating small furry animals that scurried out of their way as they turned each corner. Dunn had never seen a squirrel, but these peaceful mammal-types were well known in most human-friendly ecosystems. Though all planets were different in some respects, there was a similarity to most Concourse worlds, a similar mix of microorganisms, plants, and animals. The species were always a little different, but the larger families of animals were very close. Interbreeding of different species from separate planets had even been done, though it was rarely successful and usually looked at with disdain. To date very few organisms from one planet had proven dangerous in any way to another planet, but it was feared that toying with the delicate balances of the worlds was foolish. Still, whatever planet you happened to be on, a bear was a bear, and a dog was, in most respects, a dog. A squirrel, Dunn supposed, was a squirrel.

Of course, on planets which supported non-humans as the dominant species, the ecosystem was vastly different. How the galaxy unfolded this way was being hotly debated, and Dunn felt certain that a real answer would never be found. Just as well, he thought. Better to leave the universe alone.

Proxima Ser approached a large building, with narrow steps reaching hundreds of feet to the entrance. This structure, she decided, was different than the rest, and she imagined that in its day it was a building of great importance. "What do you say we start looking indoors, Henn? It's pretty certain that any answers we hope to get will be inside somewhere, and this place certainly looks like it was a central point of the city."

Dunn had been distracted by the opposite thought. He stood looking at a building that had suffered much greater erosion than the rest of the city, and this puzzled him. It was smaller than most of other buildings, older, built not from gleaming metal or stone, but of a plant fiber and resin that surely predated the rest of the town.

"You're right, there, Prox," he said "and I'll meet you over there in a few minutes. There's something I want to check out first." They each entered their respective doorways, satisfied that they were heading toward the answers.

Proxima Ser opened the shining metal and glass doors, glanced at the etched writing on the surface, but knew the ability to understand the Bryce language was limited to only a few of the best linguists of the Concourse, and none of those would be considered experts. Still, she recorded the image. Inside, the ravages of time were less evident. If not for a layer of dust which covered literally everything, it could open for business, she thought. Each step created a cloud at her feet which slowly settled back down as she moved along. She had entered a large room, what appeared to be a lobby of this building. The similarities to human structures was unsettling -- that is, she corrected herself, *other* human structures, since the Bryce were obviously humanoid. The room was dotted with tables and chairs, of a strange style but recognizable. To her left, along the entire wall, was a counter, and behind it more of the Bryce writing she had seen throughout the city. That this had been some type of central meeting place was obvious, but for what purpose he couldn't say. It could be a transtube station, or a scientific university - even the local food shop. She recorded and moved toward the back of the room where a small hallway seemed to lead farther into the building, and where the sunlight which had brightened the lobby failed to follow. She would need to activate her lights.

Dunn stepped into a different scene. The door was almost off its hinges, and he was careful not to move it too much or too fast. It could have been made of some type of wood, but it was much lighter, and the grain of the door seemed artificial. He stepped into a small room, long abandoned and decayed. The squirrel animals burst from their nests and scurried through broken windows, lifting a cloud of fine dust that filled the room as the breeze from outside caught it. The walls, of the same artificial wood material as he had noticed on the door, contained a series of scenes in relief. Though the specific acts depicted were foreign to him, any old spaceman could recognize pictures of deity worship. This, then, was a temple, which could explain why it had fallen into greater disrepair than the other buildings. Obviously older, the inhabitants had resisted or rejected any attempts to modernize the structure, so the elements would naturally gain a foothold much more quickly, much more severely.

Dunn moved deeper into the room, satisfied now that its differences could easily be explained. His narrow light beam played along the images on the walls, then ---

Siren!

Dunn instinctively crouched, making himself as small a target as possible. He had been caught by ancient alarm systems before, protection devices activated long after the builders were dead. It took only a second to realize the sirens were not coming from within the temple, but from outside. He bolted through the door in time to see a cluster of small ships

- six, he later realized - surrounding the large building across the way, and in time to see Proxima Ser, her hands electronically bound by a ring of energy, carried struggling to one of the ships which had landed just at the bottom of the steps. The other ships all landed in the street as the siren stopped, and from each two men emerged and ran into various structures. The ship with Ser lifted without noise and streaked away.

Dunn saw no one heading toward him, but he pulled out his pistolaser. The men he saw were unarmed, which meant they were most likely Bryce. After all, what need did they have for weapons when their mere touch caused death? Dunn remembered that those who breathed the same air as the Bryce died later, too, so he had to remain in his suit. But, he conjectured, the *Taylor* crew didn't suffer from ill effects when they visited abandoned planets of the Bryce, so this wasn't certain.

All this guessing, he suddenly realized, was useless. Ser was captured, and if he didn't get back to his ship either he, the ship, or both, would certainly be discovered. Ironically, it was curiosity of other races which the Bryce saw as reason enough to kill, but Dunn's curiosity of this old temple had probably kept him from being immediately captured. The streets were deserted. At least, they looked that way, the searchers all occupied inside. How had they been discovered? How did they know where Ser was so quickly?

He ran from the doorway, and moved along the edge of the walls, moving stealthily (he hoped) in the direction of his ship. He wanted to circumvent the center of town, but to do that he would have to go through areas he was unfamiliar with and risk getting lost. Plus, if his ship was discovered, he was surely dead. So, gun in hand, he ran straight across the street, within yards of the alien ships which stood waiting, and ducked behind a wall at the other side. His ship was close by, and he felt a surge of relief that he would make it undetected, a feeling he quickly learned was much too soon. He heard multiple voices, unfriendly voices, and then saw figures running toward him from a half dozen doorways.

Dunn sized up the situation quickly, and knew that in a straight race they would catch him before he reached his ship. He could shoot them, or some of them, but his orders didn't include killing the Bryce. Dunn took aim at one of the ships and fired. As he disappeared behind the wall the first wave of heat and concussion of air hit the Bryce pursuers, knocking them momentarily to the ground. Dunn ran at full speed toward his ship.

Inside the ship he had no time for preliminaries. How many more ships awaited him in the air or in space he didn't know. Perhaps bigger, more powerful vessels patrolled the skies. That would be unexpected, probably disastrous. He lifted off immediately at full power, and without regard for direction he hit the throttles. He cleared the atmosphere and a quick check of the sensors showed no more ships, so he powered down slightly, and took stock of the situation.

***

A few minutes earlier Proxima Ser had walked slowly through the building. She stood in a long hallway, doors on either side about ten meters apart.

To the left of each door was a viewscreen, and she imagined it was a sign, identifier of the contents of the room behind, but there was no power to light the signs - not that she would be able to understand what it said. This could be, she thought, anything from a hotel to a biological laboratory where the deadly Bryce Effect was created. If it was created at all; it could be a natural defense, though Concourse scientists and sociopsychologists resisted that conclusion.

She chose a door at random, and pushed it open. It had been secured with some type of electronic locking mechanism, but of course with no power there would be no security. The room, lit only by her beam, froze her in terror. The threat of the Bryce was real, and it was horrible.

She left the room quickly to find Dunn. As she entered the hallway she was suddenly struck by multiple bars of light from all angles. The ceiling, the floor, the very walls seems to come alive, and as the beams struck her all at once she was unable to move.

"Dunn! I'm caught in some kind of electronic security web. I must have activated it when I entered one of the labs. I need you to come set me free so I can show you what I've discovered." He would have no trouble tracking her signal, and the beams seemed to be designed to hold her, not hurt her, so she waited calmly.

Seconds later she saw movement ahead. Dunn had arrived quickly; he must have already been on his way, she thought. Then she saw another figure, and another. She shouted a warning through the comm system, then they reached her.

***

His ship was very small, and there were no signs of search or pursuit. Nonetheless Dunn chose not to remain in orbit around the planet where they had been discovered. The Bryce had come out of nowhere, so they had some sensitive tracking devices, and they had some troops in these supposedly abandoned worlds. It only deepened the mystery, and the danger.

The mission had been to gather information about the Bryce, and to avoid contact at all costs. They had succeeded in getting information, such as it was, but failed terribly in avoiding the Bryce. Worse, Ser faced an uncertain future. Perhaps she had some immunity to the Bryce Effect, but any race so intent on killing others who strayed too closely would have many other methods for killing.

Dunn's orders in this case were specific - he was to return to the Concourse if there was inadvertent contact, or even danger of contact. Ser wore nothing to indicate her origin, so the Bryce would be unlikely to determine from where she had come, but the ship would be a different story. They had been given self-destruct orders if the ship was in danger of capture, because it was decided that the ship could be traced to the Concourse. The ship, however, was not in any danger.

Dunn scanned the area once more for any sign of Bryce ships. He plotted the most direct course for the Concourse. He punched the engines to full power.

After he had traveled less than two light years, he changed course, starting a turn which would take him back toward Moogh. If necessary he would destroy the ship to prevent Concourse liability. If necessary he would die facing the Bryce. He would not abandon Proxima Ser to them.

CHAPTER FIVE
TERETANIA - CONCOURSE HEADQUARTERS
15:22:03

Three weeks after Proxima Ser was captured by the Bryce, Charles Forrester learned of the plan's failure. He also learned, to his anger and dismay, that his orders had been disobeyed. The small hydrantium module arrived undamaged, which was a stroke of luck. It was housed in a tiny ship, one only a few feet across, and launched at hyperlight speeds toward the destination. The greater the distance the greater the chance that gravitational forces would alter the small missile's course, and that it would never even come close to the goal. But the message from Dunn arrived within a couple light years of the target buoy, and its weak signal was picked up immediately. This type of communication was slow and failure rates were high, but communication over interstellar distances could be picked up by anyone, and Dunn couldn't allow the Bryce to know his plans.

Another individual rescue, Forrester thought. Yet another example of one person risking the greater good to help someone. Dunn's move was dangerous, he knew. Once the Bryce became aware of the ship it was in great danger of capture, and the Concourse couldn't afford that. Dunn was one of the Concourse's best pilots, and he obviously considered Proxima Ser to be more important than the mission. Fools! Constantly he fought against people who put individual loyalty above the loyalty to the government, to the ideals, to the survival of the Concourse. Maybe it was cold, Forrester thought. *Maybe I am cold and heartless when it comes to individuals. But that's what makes me good in this job - because I'm not responsible for one person, but for trillions. One person - any one person, even me - is expendable.*

It was the same with the Concourse Council. To each council member, the interests of their planet took priority over the interests of the Concourse as a whole. Even Garl Zavis, who had made sacrifices for the good of all, said time and again that he would protect Teretania above all else.

Ser was important, because of her immunity, because she might be the only one, and he didn't discount the value of her life, but the risk of the Bryce finding the Concourse ship, and identifying the origin, was too great. He regretted this mission. Had he chosen the wrong plan? Prior to the Battle of Teretania Forrester moved slowly, planned and waited - yes, he took action, but most of it was preparatory. The result, though to everyone else appeared successful, was disaster. His part was complete failure: He failed to build the fleet he needed; He failed to keep his plans secret from the Hybrids; He failed to infiltrate Vandettri's network; He failed to be ready for the attack. Only the sacrifice of Taylor, brought about by an amazing stroke of luck, and courage, saved them. Forrester knew his own plans, they were for nothing. Never again would he take the patient route. They needed information, and they needed it right away, but his idea had again failed.

***

This day was to be another first. He had battled Gorups, killed them, been almost killed by them, but he had never sat across a table from them to talk. Forrester's forehead dripped with sweat and his hands shook. He wasn't afraid of the Gorups -- they had proven to be the weakest of their enemies and the easiest to dictate terms to in the past -- but of all the alien races they had run across, friend or enemy, the Gorups were the most alien.

As the delegation entered the room, Forrester stood. Four Gorups walked in on lumpy, undulating gray legs. None stood more than four foot tall, their faces looked identical to Forrester; he'd never tell them apart. They looked more like large bipedal manatees, an earth creature that no one seemed to care for much. Behind the Gorups came two security guards, their riflasers drawn and ready. Forrester almost motioned them away, but thought better of it. Finally Alphan, the linguist and interpreter, and Merwa Yon entered. The atmosphere would support both species, though the oxygen content was lowered just slightly to make it more comfortable to the Gorups. Merwa Yon sat, staring with obvious hatred at the aliens. Their expression was impossible to read. The lumpy, almost formless torso of the Gorups were covered in a loose fitting tunic, something they probably wore just for this occasion, the Gorups themselves being asexual and unconcerned about such things as modesty.

Introductions were made, and Forrester tried to commit the titles to memory - there were no names offered. Alphan, her voice cracking in nervous anticipation, reported that the Gorups were prepared to share the information they had on the Bryce. This didn't surprise Forrester or Yon, since they had not long before threatened to come and get the information if it wasn't forthcoming. The carefully worded but very plain threat was no bluff.

Leader One began.

"Bryce is human but not like you. You word is xenophobe. No limits to effort to remain alone."

Forrester interrupted. "You're not telling us anything we don't already know, Leader One. You fought the Bryce, a long time ago. Tell me about that." He no longer hated the Gorups, he told himself. More pitied them.

"Yes, long ago. Bryce attacked. Our technology help, but Bryce came anyway. On planet they came, and became touchkillers."

"So you were not immune to this Bryce Effect?"

"Some were, only a few. We battled them for many years," - the translators were adapting to the speech patterns, and the thoughts came through as more complete sentences. "One of twenty was immune. Our ships were faster, stronger, but they had the touchkillers. There was going to be no winner, only the loss of most from each race. The attack ended, and they returned to their planets."

Another Gorup spoke, whom Forrester knew only as Scientist. "They have vast space, but most is left alone. They occupy one planet only, surrounded by as much emptiness as they can manage."

"Why?" Merwa Yon asked. "What makes them so afraid of everyone?"

"Unknown. The touchkillers have always been there, but for years they occupied their planets, and there was no contact at all. Suddenly one day, they were attacking."

Alphan stood. Her red tunic contrasted sharply with her deep blue skin. Forrester thought she was attractive - her short copper hair, deep purple lips, and blue skin somehow pleasing to the eye.

"I think I can fill in some of the communication gaps, based on the documents I've received from the Gorup leaders. Some of it is conjecture, but I think we can count on most of it being true enough. The Bryce developed much the same way the Concourse worlds did. They seem to have been just a little behind us technologically, but otherwise fell right in step with what seems to be the normal pace for the known galaxy." Scientists had theorized as to why most species, despite their vast differences and isolation from one another, developed with relative equality when it came to technology. The debates were hot and many, but it was a fact that no race, so far, outpaced others by more than a few decades.

"Perhaps we'll never know the reason why, but just as the human worlds here in the Concourse met with hostile races, so did the Bryce. The Gorups may have been one of those, or it may have been confined to other areas, but they faced the same situation. Here, we formed alliances where we could. There, for some reason, they chose to withdraw and isolate."

"Surely they couldn't expect to avoid contact with the rest of the galaxy that way," Yon said.

"Well, not completely. They worked on technology, and developed their Bryce Effect. This is almost certainly not a natural defense. Then they moved out into the galaxy a little bit. I think they probably destroyed a few small races, took over their worlds, and settled down. When they reached a species that could match them technologically, or outgun them enough to counteract the Bryce Effect, they stopped, withdrew for a while. Then, when they felt strong enough again, they expanded their bubble a little more. From this information and what we have learned through....other sources...this pattern went through three or four cycles. Then they found the Gorups."

"I think I am starting to understand," Forrester said. "The Gorups were more alien than races they had encountered previously. Some were immune. The Gorup empire was large, technologically equal. Suddenly the Bryce were stretched thin, and they couldn't handle the attack."

Alphan smiled. "Right. They were so used to easy victory that this resistance almost destroyed them." She turned to the Gorups. "You never ventured into Bryce space, so you couldn't know, but you had beaten them almost completely. If you had moved against them, they would have been too small in numbers to fight."

"We're not aggressive," Leader One said.

"You came at us right enough!" Yon shouted.

Alphan quickly said "Yes, they did. To the Gorups all humans seemed alike, and they didn't view their encounter with the Bryce as a victory. They were scared, and when they saw us, humanoids, progressing on their other border, they attacked. At least, that was why they attacked the first time. The Unity War of fifteen years ago was to them a battle for survival."

"That's a lie," Merwa Yon said. "I was there, just a young soldier, but I was there. I saw entire cities destroyed without a thought, entire worlds ---"

"We did to you what you - what the Bryce - did to us. We couldn't see any difference between the species."

"They waged a fierce war," Alphan said, "but it was a war of desperation. Interestingly, the Gorups were unaware that the Brodians were fighting us on another front. They barely knew that the Brodians existed. When they were beaten back, the Gorups didn't know what to do. They were, frankly, waiting to be killed by someone."

"Touchkillers," Leader One said again. "We could fight technology, but we couldn't fight touchkillers. Eventually, we thought, you would become like them. We needed immunity.

Forrester's eyes widened. "Oh my God. The Brodian-Gorup Hybrids. That was an attempt to create an immunity to the Bryce Effect."

"Yes," Scientist said, "and it was a disaster. The Hybrids took control of both races, and launched the recent war. We wanted to find a protection from the touchkillers. We found instead a race worse than the worst of us, made from us. Every Gorup is glad the Hybrids are dead."

Forrester's entire image of the Gorups changed at the meeting. They weren't, he realized, an evil empire bent on galactic domination and the destruction of humans. They were a sad, pitiful people, frightened into war and living in fear. Viewed as would-be conquerors by every Concourse world on the Gorup front, they were instead more like scurrying animals looking for a safe haven.

The rest of the meeting became a series of guesses. The Gorups feared that the Bryce would advance their technology and attack again, perhaps with stronger touchkillers. No one knew what was happening to the Bryce in other parts of the galaxy, particularly toward the galactic center. The Hybrids had been immune to the Bryce Effect, but their other frailties and their inherent hostility made the experiment a terrible failure, for the whole galactic arm. Merwa Yon was unwilling to accept the Gorups at their word. Forrester saw no problem in accepting what they said, because he no longer believed the Gorups were a threat. They didn't really have the stomach for battle. A series of guesses - and the future of everything depending on whether those guesses were right.

***

An hour later only Alphan remained, sitting at Forrester's comm panel. The oxygen level had returned to normal levels, though the difference was barely perceptible. Forrester stood over her, watching her skilled and delicate hands work the keyboard. Computers long since had moved to voice controls for most functions, but there remained subtle manipulations, illustrations, and directions for which it was necessary to show the computer rather than tell it. Alphan was particularly adept at this, and Forrester was impressed with many of her skills, which centered on language, words, and their subtle uses. He would have to be careful about what he said, he mused.

Alphan's fingers danced over the keys, decoding and translating multiple messages as they were received from the probe launched days before. With each moment she learned a little more about the Bryce language, and Forrester learned a little more about the Bryce. The probe transmitted for almost 26 hours before it stopped, for reasons unknown. Typically a probe could fail for hundreds of reasons, most completely unforeseen and not worth worrying about. The most common reason was contact with a micrometeor, a particle often too small to be seen, but which could destroy a critical relay or guidance mechanism. Logically, its failure was no cause for great concern, but Forrester found everything which had to do with the Bryce to be of great concern.

Alphan was very conscious of Forrester's proximity. She recalled when she was in complete awe of him, and perhaps she still was. He was handsome, too, for an Earther. She came to Concourse HQ straight from the top university on Letrone, excited about her opportunities to work so closely with the founder of this alliance. She left behind a family, and a suitor who could not understand her desire to leave. In the three months on Concourse HQ she moved quickly up the ladder, for she had a unique ability to decipher meaning, not just literal translations, from words. One of only a handful of Latronians at the headquarters, she had little social life, few friends, and thankfully plenty of work.

She pretended not to notice his closeness. On the screen the computer, aided by Alphan, decoded the data with great speed, to an accuracy of nearly 92%. The remaining 8% came from Alphan herself, using intuitive logic that computers still did not possess.

It was that 8% Forrester relied on the most. She told him she would be working at the computer for hours, and she knew he was tired, which he was. He moved over to the couch and closed his eyes for what seemed like seconds, though he later learned that three hours has passed before she awaken him with a gasp.

"What is it?"

Her skin, normally deep and intense blue, was pale and faded. "The Touchkillers are coming!"

Most of the messages intercepted by the probe were unimportant and barely understandable. Even when the language is known and some of the meanings inferred, without a frame of reference the conversations were mostly relevant only to the primary participants. Only one of ten messages meant anything, and only one of a hundred of those could mean anything important. But Alphan was good, and she was persistent. The 748th individual message made her suspicious. The 8,044[th] concerned her, and she nearly woke Forrester right then. But when she read the 19,219[th] message, she knew the truth - the Bryce were coming after the Concourse, with the intention of destroying it. It took only minutes to prove that to Forrester.

CHAPTER SIX
THE PLANET ALLEGHANY
15:22:08

The first ship touched down on Alleghany six minutes before Forrester learned that the attack was coming. It was the middle of the busiest day of the busiest week in the busiest city of the planet. Whether that was intended or just fortunate for the Bryce would be debated, but it made the attack more successful - or more tragic, depending on your point of view.

The modern planets of the Concourse - and there were none more modern that Alleghany - had a police force on the ground and military in the air to prevent unauthorized landings practically anywhere on the planet. Additionally, the Concourse Defense Force had a sizable fleet in the area, just in case the Gorups or some other unfriendly entity wanted to launch an attack. The finely-tuned sensors of the fleet could detect weapons systems long before a ship approached. Interceptors from the Alleghany military would keep any ship from making its way to the surface. If those were unsuccessful, the well-trained police would meet them at the ground. All of these defenses were among the best in the Concourse arsenal, but because the nature of the Bryce was unheard of, the defenses were useless.

The ships approached unmolested because, although large, they showed no weapons systems of any kind. There was curiosity, some concern, but no action taken. When the massive ships entered orbit and thousands of smaller ships began pouring from multiple hangars, an alarm was sounded, but no worthwhile action was possible because the number of ships dwarfed any force ready to meet them.

Five empty shells orbited the planet, as twenty thousand tiny one-man craft dropped into the atmosphere. Planetary shields were small, expensive, and almost impossible to maintain in a commercial and political society such as Alleghany, so as the ships scattered across the surface, and Bryce left their ships to the surprise of millions of citizens, almost none were stopped.

The attack consisted merely of existence. The Bryce walked down the streets, nothing more. At first the only Alleghanians to die were those close to the Bryce, but as minutes passed those breathing the air nearby were overcome. Age, sex, income or political power meant nothing. Citizens and police, alarmed at the visions before their eyes and aware that these strange beings were the cause, killed many Bryce - but that didn't stop the death as even the corpse was lethal.

Within an hour no part of the planet Alleghany remained uncontaminated. In the panic many were evacuated, some successfully, others not as the poisonous Bryce Effect entered their ships before take-off. The Bryce agents - men, women, and children - never tried to return to their ships, and never tried to defend themselves against any attack. For them it seemed being on the surface, dead or alive, was enough.

The first clue that not all people were affected by this airborne death came from those ships which carried the Bryce Effect on board. Much as with *The Taylor*, death was slower, but just as definite, for most of the crew. On some ships, however, a few survived - one out of a thousand, according to the best guesses.

Carefully quarantined until the air around them was clean, these survivors, numbering a few hundred, were transported to Concourse HQ on Teretania. Based on these numbers, another 50,000 possibly remained alive on Alleghany, immune to the Bryce Effect, but unreachable by anything the Concourse had available.

Central Control for Concourse HQ was normally manned by eight or ten technicians, handling mostly routine matters. Now it held over fifty, and the atmosphere bordered on panic. Shulman, communications technician, approached Charles Forrester. He noticed how disheveled Forrester looked, the lines of worry intensified by the serious and sad expression in his eyes. Shulman waited for a lull in the conversation.

"I have confirmation from General Monroc that the Bryce vessels have been destroyed," he said.

Forrester didn't answer right away. He surveyed the room. Concourse Central Control was a two-level semi-circle. A row of consoles lined the bulkheads most of the way around the curve on the top, overlooking the main floor seven feet below. Six separate computer consoles occupied the curve of the semi-circle, and at least one man operated each device. In the center of the curve sat one of the four exits, just at the top of the stairs that led to the level. Opposite, along the back wall, three technicians each manned two longer consoles. Another two exits were available on that wall, and another set of steps leading to that area. Beneath the railing on the lower floor, less space was allocated to machines and more to man. Two large banks of control boards faced each other, large and complex enough that eight different men were needed to keep it monitored. Most of the main floor was being used for meeting and arguing about the current crisis. Forrester stood at the head of a rectangular plastic table, painted orange and completely out of place in this sea of lights and metal. Some men were seated along each side, and others sat at one of the three benches which had been brought in and scattered where space would permit. There was only one exit on this level, a tunnel which skirted beneath the upper level and led directly to Forrester's offices. There was no main viewscreen to monitor anything going on outside, but each of the control boards could display any information needed, and that gave over a dozen different viewports.

Right now there was nothing to see, only information to digest. The population of Alleghany had been decimated. The Bryce attackers were stranded on the planet, and it was likely that most or all would be killed by the surviving Alleghanians, or blown from the skies if they tried to reach their now-destroyed carrier ships. So far none had tried. Finally Forrester looked up. "Thank you," was all he said.

Forrester turned to one of the computer technicians. "I need to know what route the Bryce took to reach Allegheny. Did they come directly through Gorup space, or did they go around it? More importantly, I need to know if there were other ships with them, ships which could have moved on other Concourse planets." The general alarm had gone out, and it was unlikely that any unidentified ship would get within a light year of a Concourse planet now. But the threat remained real.

As if in answer to his question the battle alarms of Teretania suddenly screamed.

"Sir!" came the cry from one of his lieutenants. "Sensors indicate the approach of a large vessel, type and source unknown." Forrester ran to the console, saw the data streaming across the screen. He could interpret the information reasonably well, but it was coming by too quickly.

"I'm going to my office, where I can see something! And tell someone to get a real viewscreen in here!" He ran through the passageway. As he flew through the door to his office the lights came on. "Computer, viewscreen on, exterior view!"

The computer acknowledged VIEWSCREEN ON.

Forrester saw a vessel, and although he had no frame of reference, he instinctively knew it must be a Bryce ship. The Teretanian defenses were already beginning, but before her big guns could be trained on the ship, huge doors opened and thousands of smaller vessels poured out, like angry bees from a disturbed hive. The large ship was quickly destroyed, but the small ships swarmed the surface of Teretania, searching, he knew, for some method of breaking through the hull. They used no weapons that Forrester could see. Despite the element of surprise, there seemed little danger that the Bryce would infiltrate the ship. He called Zavis.

"Garl, how did that ship sneak up on us?"

"We don't have a clue. Suddenly it was there, as if it popped out of nothingness. I suppose any race so intent on secrecy might find a way to approach undetected. If so, there could be more."

Forrester sat at his desk, and looked up at the large viewscreen which showed Teretanian fighters emerging from their bays to fight the Bryce.

"Garl, stop the attack! Don't open your bays to send out fighters!"

"That's impossible Charles. We have to go after them. We had our ships trapped once before, you remember, in the when the Hybrids attacked. We won't let that happen again."

"You don't understand. There's no way the Bryce can get inside the ship, except through the fighter bays when your ships attempt to leave. Otherwise we're immune unless they have some other weapons, and there's no indication of that. You have to call them back."

Garl Zavis was distracted momentarily, and then Forrester heard him stop the fighters from returning. "You're right, Charles," he said "We've had three reports of Bryce ships flying into the bays as ships attempted to leave. They weren't trying to stop the emerging ships and didn't seem concerned with surviving the attempt, just opening up a hole. We have two breaches, but we'll have them closed in a few minutes."

"I know you have some ships out there now," Forrester said, "but you can't bring them back as long as there are Bryce out there. You'll have to try to use your automatic guns to pick the Bryce off one at a time. They aren't very good this close to the ship, but you cannot risk letting them in by trying to recall your pilots."

Forrester switched off the comm panel. Zavis didn't need Forrester looking over his shoulder right now. He suddenly felt helpless. Forrester controlled the Concourse fleet, but very little of that was here on Teretania. Zavis was responsible for protecting the ship, and although he made an initial error in evaluating the best way to defend against the Bryce attack, Forrester had to trust that he would repair the damage. Forrester had no choice, because Teretania wasn't his to control.

The reports came in slowly. Alphan, and Forrester led the group that sifted through the communications as they filtered in from Concourse planets. Six planets, plus Teretania, had been attacked. All sustained great loss of life. Those who had a little warning were able to destroy some of the Bryce ships before they left their mother vessel, and so far the devastation on those planets was less. It appeared that the Bryce Effect was all a matter of concentration. Whatever caused the death dissipated to a non-lethal level over time and space, and although the Bryce themselves were still fatal to the touch after death, they could be disposed of in fire. The limited information showed that their breath and their touch were the most dangerous factors. It helped to know this, but only a little. They learned that a total of 22 ships formed the attack convoy, and that they took a long circuitous route far below the galactic plane. Assuming Bryce ship speed was comparable to that of the Concourse, such a trip had to take at least three weeks. The attack had been planned for a while. Were more on the way? The Gorups, to this point, had been avoided by the Bryce. Was this because the Gorups were not a perceived threat, or were the Bryce concerned about angering the Gorups? At this point there was no way to know.

"We have to assume more attacks are coming," Monroc said.

"Not necessarily," Alphan replied. "Their pattern has never been to skip past a species or territory to attack what is beyond. This is something new for them. I could be wrong, but this might have been nothing more than a stay-away warning."

Monroc asked, "The destruction of most of six planets, and the attack on the Concourse HQ itself, just a warning?"

"Certainly, from their perspective, I mean. Look at the situation. The Bryce are not expansionists, not by any definition. They have, over the past three or four centuries, done only what was necessary - in their minds - to create a buffer zone between their world and the rest of the galaxy. We may not understand their motives, or be able to grasp their paranoia, but their methods are plain. They only crossed the interstellar void when they felt the Gorups were a threat, and they correctly judged when it was again safe to withdraw. To attack the Concourse and take it to the point of surrender or defeat, would be enclosing the Gorups in their buffer zone, something they are never going to do. And they have to know that moving deeper into this stellar area, the galactic spur in which the Concourse sits, would certainly bring them into greater contact, since the concentration of stellar systems is greater on the far side of the Concourse - that's if we assume they even know how large or small the Concourse is. They may have still just attacked as a warning, to make sure we did what the Gorups did - left them alone."

Forrester said, "Didn't you say, when we first received the warning from their buoy, that they threatened to destroy the species that invaded their territory?" He gave her a slight smile. He didn't want to put her on the spot, but someone was bound to ask the question, and better it come from him than from Yon or one of the others.

"Sure, but the nature of threats is to make crossing the buoy completely unacceptable. Had they said 'If you cross we will send a group of ships to attack you and warn you off' that would not have been strong enough."

"It wasn't going to be strong enough a warning, no matter what, was it?" Merwa Yon said loudly from a distance.

Yon had been standing in the back of the room, but moved through the crowd with a quick three steps and turned to face them. Eleven others besides Forrester, Alphan, and Yon stood speechless to this point, and all eyes were on Yon, anticipating what he wanted to say. These were leading members of the Concourse Council, including ambassadors from three of the six planets that had been attacked.

"Millions of lives have been lost already," he said, "because we ignored the warning."

"We didn't know its purpose until later," Forrester said.

"That's right, we didn't know its purpose, but we went ahead anyway, and the crew of the Taylor died. Except Proxima Ser, who is as we speak lost, captured, or killed on the Bryce home planet." Forrester took a step toward Yon, to remind him that he was talking about confidential matters, but he stopped himself, knowing it was too late now to prevent the disclosure, and looking like that's what he wanted to do would only make matters worse.

"I sent them there," Forrester said. "We needed more information; the warning buoy was both threatening and unclear. We needed information. As

Director I have the authority to send a reconnaissance mission."

Yon seemed to smile for a second, but then his face went serious. "But that wasn't all you did, was it, Mr. Director? You sent other probes as well. Secretly."

Forrester was stunned. He had concerns about Yon, but to hear him talk openly about Concourse Intelligence tactics in front of the council - it was incredible. "We sent an unmanned probe, yes. It has provided information, and there's nothing to indicate that it was detected by the Bryce."

"No? What about the attack? That indicates something to me --"

The room erupted in multiple conversations. Two council members cornered Forrester. He defended his acts, talked about the need for information, and promised that he had not exceeded his authority. He brought these people to his office to discuss their next step in the war that had just begun, but now he was forced to defend his actions, forced to defend that he hadn't done anything to provoke the attack.

Or had he?

Forrester reclaimed control of the room by using him comm system to amplify his voice. "Everything the Concourse and this office has done has been within the law and in the best interests of Concourse safety. This is not the time to discuss any possible errors. We are at war, and our one and only focus right now needs to be what action we'll take next."

The room quieted. Some people left, including Merwa Yon.

Forrester's conversation later that day with Garl Zavis was equally uncomfortable. Twenty pilots had been killed during the Bryce attack. A few died when their ships were rammed by Bryce vessels, but others merely ran out of fuel and life support before the Bryce did. The damage to Teretania was minimal, but the effects of the attack were great. Zavis didn't directly question Forrester's actions, but the tension in the air was noticeable. They agreed to move the ship a little deeper into Concourse territory, for now.

Merwa Yon went to the media, and by the next day the vid and the comm systems were flooded with reports of the probes and spy missions sent into Bryce territory. Some were supportive, accepting the perspective and agreeing to the idea that the need for information about possible enemies was paramount. After all, hadn't the Concourse been attacked by secret enemies before? Of course, the other reports pointed out, Forrester had information about those other attacks prior to the day they took place, and he kept that information from the Concourse people. How much was he planning to reveal this time? Members of the Concourse Council called for a removal hearing against Forrester. It was defeated by a 2/3 majority, but that it was even suggested, and garnered votes from over a dozen worlds, was telling.

Forrester would not normally, during time of war, spend time talking with the media. He didn't disdain them; he merely would not have thought it was proper at the time, that it was not at that moment a priority. But those votes in the council chambers changed everything. The Concourse had a battle with the Bryce, a very dangerous and still unknown enemy.

Forrester suddenly had a battle of his own - a fight to retain his job.

By the time a day had passed, Forrester was exhausted. He'd used every vid and comm channel, called in every supporter he had and favor he was owed, and as he settled into his quarters he felt reasonably comfortable that the damage done by Merwa Yon - at least the damage he was aware of - had been minimized. Forrester sent an official notice to Yon that he was no longer a Concourse officer, though this was only a formality. He scheduled a meeting of his generals for the morning, and reached his bed unable to stand another minute. If he slept that night, he could not recall it.

CHAPTER SEVEN
CONCOURSE HEADQUARTERS
15:22:22

Within two weeks the survivor studies had been set up. A cross-section of volunteers who proved immune to the Bryce Effect were housed, cared for, studied, and risked in the laboratory. The best estimates suggested that almost one in 1200 people were immune, and there had to be a reason, one which could be understood, exploited. The main section of the lab was completely cut off from the rest of the headquarters, and of course the ship population. Air samples, soil samples, and Bryce corpses were all necessary segments of the study, and the danger of contamination was seriously considered. Zavis didn't want the studies on the ship, but with more Bryce attacks happening, there was no place more secure than the Teretania's forium hull.

Forrester played the media. He talked with his generals, scientists, and advisors. The Bryce surprised them and continued to attack, though only one planet at a time, and the effects were lessened. Most of the Bryce ships were destroyed before they could reach the planetary systems. But some ships got through, and some people died. Alphan and the other social scientists who predicted that the Bryce attack was a one-time event, a warning, had been wrong. Forrester's assurances of safety were shown faulty. Merwa Yon, now a private citizen, continued to embroil the media and make statements damaging to the Concourse. Forrester considered Yon's motives. Was he setting himself up as a candidate for Director? If so, why did he only hint at Concourse improprieties? Why didn't he come right out and tell people that there was a Hybrid among the Teretanian government, and that Forrester knew about it? Why didn't he tell more of the secrets that he could use? Did Yon fear Forrester would kill him? The thought had crossed his mind, but he already faced too many political and public issues - suspicion of political murder was something he didn't need to add to the mix.

Alphan stayed with him from time to time. They were lovers now, Forrester's first serious relationship in many years. She was young, not much more than a girl despite her intelligence and instinct. She trusted Forrester completely, and never questioned him. Her youth and her admiration made their relationship easy for him. He loved her innocence, her naivete. He considered that he might be taking advantage of that innocence, but realized that if there was any ulterior motive in his growing desire and love for her, it was jealousy. He wished he could be more like her - able to see the best in the worst of people, and willing to trust.

The new reports of Bryce attacks were puzzling. The first attack was thrown at the planets closest to Gorup, and therefore to Bryce, space. But the new attacks, though smaller and less successful, came from every direction. The number of ships in any one attack remained small enough that tracing their path to the source was impossible. The intensity of the attacks was steady, but the number was increasing. The war had continued, and gotten worse. The Concourse planets were paralyzed. The Gorups were shaking in their formless skins. The Brodians refused to communicate. The races not yet part of the

Concourse stood afraid to be linked with it, in case the Bryce should "misunderstand." Not long ago the Concourse had few friends, but many enemies. Now she had only one enemy, but no friends. To a growing segment of the Concourse, Forrester was to blame.

He knew they could be right.

The lowest moment in recent weeks happened when there was an unknown visitor at the door. His secretary allowed the man in, so Forrester had nothing to fear. The man handed Forrester a simple piece of paper. Paper was still used, though mostly for official documents, so it didn't surprise him at all to find that he was being summoned to appear before the Concourse Council ---- for a Hearing of Removal.

CHAPTER EIGHT
CONCOURSE COUNCIL CHAMBERS
15:22:24

"Everything I have done has been within the law, and in the best interests of the Concourse."

Forrester addressed the Council President, but his image was projected to the entire Concourse Council, the gallery, and on millions of vid screens throughout the entire Concourse.

Hundreds crowded into the gallery far above the chamber floor. The representatives of the 48 Concourse planets had their seats in a semi circle around the chamber floor. The current membership filled four tiers of seats, with a fifth tier left empty for future members. Forrester stood alone on the floor, facing the raised platform, his back to the membership and audience. In front of him stood only the Council President at his podium, and Merwa Yon, his former Chief of Intelligence and Security and the man who convinced the council to hold this hearing. Yon sat calmly at a desk to the president's left. On the screen above them both Forrester saw himself, many times life-sized, testifying in defense.

Concourse law allowed for the council to remove the Director for actions which endangered the safety of the Concourse. It had been part of the charter since the government was formed over fifteen years before, but had never been used, not even after the Battle of Teretania. Forrester had deceived the populace and the council, violated Concourse law, embezzled funds and committed other more serious crimes during those days, but when the story came out the people were so relieved to be out of danger, and so proud that they had been victorious that no one could muster support for a hearing. Now there was new reason to worry, and in light of the Bryce attack, plenty of opportunity to second guess decisions and look for scapegoats. At least, that's what Forrester told himself.

Not long ago the Concourse was an unstable government, the different worlds unable to cooperate well enough to defend against the threats they faced. Forrester understood that, and took the only course he saw open, right or wrong. It was his duty. When *The Taylor* moved toward the center of the galaxy, he felt certain that finding out what lay beyond the known boundaries was the best method of protecting the Concourse. When the Bryce were found, and shown to be a potential threat, he thought he had been proven correct, and that this justified more intelligence. The arguments against him today were that had Forrester left well enough alone, had the Bryce been ignored and the Concourse paid attention to her internal issues, the terrible attacks would not have happened. Didn't they understand, though, that not knowing about the nature of their enemies had nearly destroyed the Concourse once? That the Bryce would have been there eventually, whether Forrester had looked for them or not?

"This hearing," President Feld-Mont said, "is not merely to determine the legality of your actions, but their wisdom. If you were deemed to have acted outside the law, our choice would be clear. But even within the law there are acts which constitute a danger. The council advised you in the past that perhaps it was to soon to explore beyond our borders. It would appear that advice was correct, and the membership respectfully must consider whether those acts warrant removal from office."

President Feld-Mont, tall, dark-skinned humanoid of the planet Cyllia, waved his arm in a wide arc to indicate the entire room as he said the word "membership." His election over Enoi just a week before bolstered the isolationists, and this hearing gave him a new forum to espouse the conservative views. Forrester would have preferred to see someone else in the presidential office, but he hadn't found Feld-Mont difficult to deal with on most matters.

"Mr. President, respectfully, I agree that my actions were against the advice of the council. In light of recent attacks I cannot say that the reconnaissance helped us to prepare for the Bryce well enough. But it would be premature to assume that these actions in any way precipitated the attacks on our worlds. The purpose of these missions was to learn about the Bryce, and ---"

The interruption came from the membership behind Forrester. The camera shifted almost immediately and Forrester looked at the larger-than-life image of Himdelon, ambassador from Celrone, one of the planets devastated by the first Bryce attack.

"We learned about the Bryce as they swept down and killed most of our population, Mr. Forrester! What good was your information mission to the hundreds of millions who died? How do we know that they weren't responding to your acts? How do we know?"

A general murmur echoed through the membership, and their heads nodded in agreement.

Forrester spoke now not to the President, but directly to the camera imbedded in the screen above. "We don't know - not yet, at least. The Bryce were a completely unknown race, and we might learn that it was better not to have tried to learn about them. But how could this have been predicted, by me or by anyone? And if we had waited a year, two years, or longer before venturing beyond our known borders, what then? Not having encountered the Bryce, we certainly would not have been any better prepared for them in the future than we are today. Were we to simply do nothing, and wait for the rest of the galaxy to seek us out? We did that years ago, after the so-called Unity War. It fostered enemies, and these enemies tried very hard to exploit our fears. We cannot afford to have secret enemies. We cannot avoid finding enemies in the galaxy, a galaxy much more populated and much more diverse than we would have imagined even fifty years ago. But hopefully we can find enough friends."

The questions continued, Forrester answered them in the most direct manner. After a while the questions started to repeat, and Forrester felt he would survive the day. He had convinced them that the Bryce attacks, even if based on his missions of exploration, were probably inevitable. He used the Unity War and the Battle of Teretania to fullest advantage. After each of these conflicts he was absolved of wrongdoing and hailed as a hero. Just enough of the legend survived to overshadow their fears - and perhaps the truth? The difficulties were not over, however. The Izarian ambassador startled the membership with a proposal, one which Forrester had no doubt came from the lips of Merwa Yon:

"Resolved: That a committee of three be appointed to inquire into the disastrous attacks by the Bryce, and the events leading to it, with power to send for papers and persons."

The committee, by the time the sessions ended, had been expanded to seven, and powers broadened to include all Concourse activities which related to the Bryce. This Committee of the Conduct of the War would have the power to question all Concourse citizens, and report to the council on a regular basis. Forrester doubted the true legality of the committee, but as it was merely an observing body, with no actual power, he declined to fight against it. The council chose its committee members: four ambassadors, two independent scientists, and Merwa Yon.

The gallery cheered the Council. The council itself left satisfied that Forrester was still effective, yet under tighter control. Merwa Yon, obviously, received power he felt he didn't have as Forrester's aide. Forrester just wondered where it would all lead. The infighting and distrust which plagued the Concourse Council through its earlier years had given way to more single-mindedness. But was it a conservative mind, one which could cripple the decision-making process? Time would tell, but how much time would the Bryce allow?

CHAPTER NINE
THE PLANET EARTH
15:22:22

When Rodney Barnhart sailed he did everything possible to isolate himself: no vid, no phone, nothing. For those two weeks every summer he remained alone, and each year it was harder and harder to return. Only his family drew him back. They couldn't live in isolation, so he braved the confusion of civilization for them.

He hadn't seen so much as a plane during the last few days, although that fact didn't register until he reached the docks and knew immediately something was terribly wrong. As he discovered bodies, though he had no clue as to what had afflicted them, the lack of rescue personnel told him to get home at all costs. Fear gripped him, but he had to reach his family. The decay had only started; what happened was recent. He considered it could have been disease, but whatever killed the people did it quickly, since many were still in their transport cars or engaged in business. He maneuvered his car down the cluttered roads, at times barely making a way through the obvious signs of panic and desperation. Dogs, cats, and therrills scampered across the streets, eliminating the possibility of a toxic spill. How widespread was the devastation? He rounded the corner of the block where he lived and glimpsed a figure disappearing behind a building. He jumped from the car and tried to catch up with the person, but they moved too quickly for him. He wasn't alone, that much was certain. But where were the police, the rescue teams? This happened at least a day or two before, and he seemed unaffected. Certainly they would know it was safe to enter the city.

Fear clutched at him again when he considered what the lack of outside help really meant. There might not be an outside to help.

His walked carefully up the steps of the old structure and reached his door. There was no rush. He had to know, but he didn't want to see.

Prepared for the agony of finding his family, he didn't know what to do when they weren't there. What time did this happen? He looked out the window at the streets again. Daytime, perhaps afternoon from the activity. Certainly before dinner. The traffic, the positioning of the vendors, even details he could not consciously identify told him that this happened in the middle of the day. Could his family be elsewhere in the city? Could they have escaped?

For the rest of the day Rodney searched the city, every place his wife and daughters might have visited. Twice more he saw movement he guessed was a human figure, but he was never close enough to call out.

The sun set, and the ships arrived. Without warning Rodney saw them from the North, a row of battle tanks a hundred feet above the ground. He stood in the center of the street and waved his arms - there was a rescue mission! Suddenly a blast from the ship threw him to the ground. Another blast, closer than the first, electrified the air around him. Thoughts of rescue and answers gave way to shock and panic as Rodney scrambled to his feet and stumbled, falling as much as running, into the nearest building. He burst through the door and headed for the stairs. Unless they destroyed the entire building he might have a chance to hide, at least until he could find a weapon, or learn why he was being hunted.

"Damn, missed him!" Corporal Horner yelled. He kept his sights trained on the doorway in case the figure returned to the street. From his earpiece he heard the voice of Lt. Terry.

"Horner, what's the matter with you? Didn't you see him try to wave us down? You idiot, that wasn't a Bryce! That was a survivor!"

Horner turned off the gun. "I didn't see it, Sir. Hell, there hasn't been a survivor found in two days. How was I to know?"

"You're supposed to look at what you're shooting at....*Private*. Tell you what. You go down there and get him. If he is still alive and you can get him in the ship, I might not bust you down. Now, get down there!"

In less than an hour Rodney Barnhart was on his way to the survivor camp, where his family waited for him. Corporal Horner kept his rank.

***

CONCOURSE HEADQUARTERS

Reports flowed in almost constantly now, new battles and more deaths. Every planet of the Concourse faced attack. Most attacks were small in scale, relatively, a dozen craft or so trying to slip through the heightened defenses. Most were shot down. A few got through, and people died. Even on Teretania attempts were made to break through, but so far no more Teretanians had fallen prey. Space flight was greatly restricted, and on every world homeland security was incredibly tight.

Forrester met with his top generals in Central Control. His news was not good.

"We sent a fleet toward the Bryce homeworld, one which is capable of completely emptying the planet of life, if need be. We didn't want to do it, but if that's what it took to eradicate the threat, I was prepared to give the order. The plan was to send a strong force, but keep enough behind to aid the planetary defenses in repelling any attacks. What we didn't count on were for the attacks to continue as they have, seemingly from every direction. We thought the Bryce attacked as a warning, but while the attacks have become smaller, they are more frequent. Whether that means they have fewer resources we don't know, but given our errors in the past, we would be foolish to make that assumption. Here's the reason:"

Forrester manipulated the console in front of him. Two feet above the table an image formed. Swirling lights coalesced, moving from formless photons into recognizable shapes. The men and women in the room understood the three-dimensional representation of the Concourse and surrounding areas. The systems and surrounding space which formed the Concourse were enveloped in a transparent yellow light. The Gorup space was highlighted blue, and the Brodian areas red. Where the Bryce were known to be, this was enveloped in a green light. Eyes widened and jaws opened as more green areas came into view.

"As you can see," Forrester continued, "based on our latest and best intelligence, and back-tracking

Bryce ships as best we can, we now know that the Bryce occupy more areas of space in our galactic neighborhood. The area in the Sagittarius galactic arm toward the center of our galaxy remains the largest area known, and we suspect still represents their homeworld, but they have planets - or even a series of planets - in at least five other locations: Two in the Perseus arm toward the outer rim of the galaxy, one on either side of us on the outer rim of our own galactic spur, and another in a small cluster of stars well outside the boundaries of the Orion Spur. There could be others, we don't know." He removed the image from the room. They weren't surrounded, but with pockets of Bryce on all sides, and the Bryce's fanatic efforts to attacks Concourse planets, it was close enough. "Alphan has more information about their network."

Alphan had been standing off to the side, but stepped forward. Not long ago she would have been unable to function in a crowd of such important and powerful people, but in recent weeks she found she had no choice but to forget her shyness and focus on the task at hand.

"We know that the Bryce are communicating, because the attacks are coordinated from each of the six pockets. We don't know how they are communicating, because we've intercepted nothing from these areas, not even coded messages, and they appear to have developed some method which works more quickly and more efficiently than anything we currently use."

"What is the extent of their military strength?" asked General Smith, of Earth.

Forrester said, "They are still using only the Bryce Effect, and seem willing to sacrifice their troops in every case. The number of ships attacking has been steady, averaging 130 ships from each pocket per week, but occurring at random times and toward random targets. Until we know more, I have recalled the fleet which we sent toward the Bryce homeworld." This created a stir from the group. "Destroying their ability to attack from just one pocket would reduce their strength by less than 20%. Given those numbers, defense of the planets is our first priority. The bulk of the fleet will be dispersed to the member worlds. It creates a risk from other potential threats to have the fleet so spread out, but there's no choice."

A voice from the edge of the room interrupted the murmur which followed. "So, we're going to do nothing to attack and wipe out this threat?" Venge, ambassador from the planet Complet, moved toward the group. He had remained unnoticed to this point. He was one of the seven-member Committee on the Conduct of the War (which had come to be known simply as the War Committee), created by the council to be its eyes and ears during the conflict. He stood almost seven feet tall, thin and bony even for a Completion, the wrinkled face and deep sunk eyes testament to his age and service.

"Ambassador Venge," Forrester said. "I didn't notice you there. No, it would be wrong to say that we're going to do nothing at all. We've just discovered that the Bryce are not centrally located, and that we might not be aware of all their cells. Focusing our attack on one place, a place very far away, puts too great a risk of successful attack on other planets."

"But if we went at each Bryce planet full force, and destroyed them one planet at a time, certainly it would be successful."

General Monroc stepped forward. "I am normally in favor of a full assault, but the Bryce homeworld is very far away. Mr. Forrester, why don't we split the fleet into six parts? They've shown no ability to resist, and even on six fronts we should prevail. We were willing to send sixty thousand ships to one battle front. Sending ten thousand to six fronts is the same."

"That is logical," said Venge, "and more practical than merely waiting for an attack to come, or keeping our people held hostage."

Forrester tried to keep the room calm. Although his frustration grew, he spoke slowly and calmly. "Within the last two days we learned that the Bryce were more numerous than we thought, and cover a much larger area than previously believed. We also know that they have a communications systems faster and more efficient than ours. On top of all that, they've shown a willingness to sacrifice countless thousands of lives to kill one of us, while we work extremely hard - and rightly so - to protect even one life. We have to assume that they know the strength of our fleet and where it is going. If there are more Bryce pockets, or if they are willing to simply evacuate their planets, as they have shown a willingness to do, we might never be able to catch them if we start chasing them across the galaxy. While we're spreading our fleet to the four winds they could easily be using everything they have to assault our worlds. We need to know more before we can attack. We need to build the fleet stronger, but we need to stay close to home.

"It's the conclusion of our scientists and a large number of military strategists that the key to victory – and in fact possibly the only way to win – is to find a solution to the Bryce Effect, and to protect the member worlds as best we can until that is found. They are too numerous, too spread out, and too mysterious to defeat in direct combat – yet."

Venge argued against the plan, as did some of the generals in the room. Forrester didn't need their approval, but he desperately needed their loyalty. Military minds could conceive of a medical solution, but seldom had the patience to search for it. Political minds understood the value, but lacked the scope to see beyond their borders. When the meeting ended, he felt he only had half their support, and some of that very tentative. The Meds had better show some promise, and soon.

***

When Garl Zavis entered his office that day, he was unaware of the problems Forrester faced with his generals and the new War Committee, and although he was too wise to feel relaxed, he had no reason to think that this day would be a bad one. He was quickly wrong.

The most widely read newspaper on Teretania (called newspapers even though they had long since stopped being made of any organic matter) started with a headline that turned his stomach:

HYBRIDS HIDE IN TERETANIAN GOVERNMENT

Two years ago, even a year ago, such a report wouldn't have worried him, because sightings of Hybrids were common, and very few were believed or investigated. Now, to reach the front page, a story would get serious attention. He read the article. An anonymous source cited an unnamed government official with first hand knowledge that a high-ranking member of the Teretanian government was a Hybrid. It was true, of course, Zavis thought. Weeks ago there had been rumors that a Hybrid was being held by the Concourse. That was nothing to worry about. Even a report that there was a Hybrid inside the Teretanian-controlled portions of the ship would not have bothered him so much. But this hit close to the mark. This was too accurate. The only thing missing was a name.

His wife's name.

Zavis made his decision and put down his paper in the same motion. He looked in the mirror. He wore a three-piece suit of dark green, in the conservative mode of Teretania these days. It wasn't an official call he was about to make, so an official uniform wouldn't be needed. He snapped the comm on his wrist, and left the office through his private doorway. It led through a series of doors and bulkheads around the offices. In an emergency the walls would move and the various doors would change lock-codes, providing Zavis an escape from his office in the event of terrorist attack or other emergency in the office. That day it deposited him not far from the main taxiway.

Teretania remained too large to govern in one piece, so it was divided into fourteen distinct sections. Although the boundaries were arbitrary, in the three years since the old ship was abandoned in favor of this new vessel, each of the districts had developed its own personality, its own specialty. His governmental offices were housed in the Meldron sector, named after a mythical character from early Teretania history. The man Meldron, according to legend, held a collapsing bulkhead together with his bare hands while others tried to repair the breach. Thousands were saved, the story goes, but Meldron was lost. Zavis doubted the story, but heroes were rare, and what could it hurt to honor the idea? Meldron sector exhibited most of the characteristics of a governmental seat - conservatism, arrogance, and a lack of real emotional expression. As he hailed the taxi which was needed to traverse the huge courtyard and take him to where he could pick up the series of lifttubes and slidewalks, he looked around. Most districts had one or more of these massive open spaces, bordered for story after story by businesses and offices. The Meldron mallspace stood fifty-three stories tall, and from where Zavis stood looking over the railing, it went above and below him until it faded into a blurry set of lights and motion. Taxis carried people from one shop level to another, from one office to another. A person could merely walk the perimeter of each level, take stairs or lifttubes to get from one level to another, but with over 3000 shops scattered over miles of shipspace, it was much easier to grab a taxi and use the on-board computer to locate what you wanted. The drivers often knew more than the computers - but not always.

A blue taxi pulled up alongside Zavis, and a portly man shouted,"Where to, buddy?" Zavis quickly got into the car before anyone on the level could recognize him, and asked the driver to take him to the opposite side, the best place to continue to the Freedom sector. The driver indicated no recognition of Zavis, and only when he smiled about that did Zavis realize that he would receive some serious criticism from his office staff for leaving without notice and without escort. He closed the window between him and the driver and called his office on his Comm. They wouldn't be any happier he was out alone, but at least they wouldn't panic when they discovered he was gone.

He reached the other side a few minutes later, paid the driver with a modest tip, and joined the morning commuters on the Freedom-bound slidewalk. The slidewalk was the most common form of mass transit on Teretania, and the ship contained thousands of miles of these conveyors. Ten feet wide, with endless rows of seats on the right side of the belts for those who choose, it also allowed people on the left to walk as they rode along, either to increase their speed and reach their destination more quickly, or for simple exercise. Zavis sat, his face buried in a vid screen, still hoping to finish his journey without being recognized.

A little more than three years ago Zavis had been acting President of the old ship, a massive but decrepit hulk. The term Hybrid, as a race, was unknown. The Concourse was a necessary evil. He conspired with Forrester to defraud and deceive everyone, because Zavis believed he had no other choice. Had he refused to allow Forrester to build the secret fleet and hide it on the newly-constructed Teretania-2, as it had been called then, he believed that the Hybrid threat, as revealed by Forrester, would have conquered the human worlds. In the end the secret fleet mattered little and all their plans merely played into the hand of their enemies, bringing death and destruction closer, more quickly. Only unbelievable luck, and the willingness of Ian Taylor to sacrifice his life, saved them. He hated Forrester in those days, and when he was certain both men would be arrested and imprisoned for their crimes, he wanted nothing more than the chance to kill Forrester. Amazingly, their plan was perceived as being successful, the crimes forgiven, and the power of both men increased.

Now he trusted Forrester, and welcomed the Concourse. Zavis' arrogance and Teretanian pride, he thought, had been costly. Teretania, for all her marvels, was nothing without the other Concourse worlds. She had been the target of the Hybrids while under the protection of the Concourse, and surely without the Concourse she would be an easy prey for any race who wished to take it over, or destroy it.

He understood the enemies outside the confines of the ship. Within the hulls, though, there remained trouble. Political factions wanted different relationships between Teretania and the Concourse worlds. Some sought economic advantages, bigger profits on commercial runs. Others resented Concourse interference, and sought the removal of Concourse Headquarters from the ship. Small but militant factions looked for more extreme measures, some of which included the removal of Zavis from office, by force if necessary. In fact, he thought, he was perhaps foolish to come out here alone, despite his overall popularity. It only took one blaster, one shot. Could one of these political factions be behind the stories about Hybrids? If so, why not use Canthay's name? Surely anyone with this information would know who it was they wrote about. Or was this a more subtle plot? If so, he was making the right move for himself, but perhaps also the move the creators of this story wanted him to make.

Twenty minutes later he reached the front offices of Bren Cahill. Cahill owned and published the paper which ran the article that brought him here, as well as vid and comm stations on Teretania. Possibly Cahill knew little or nothing about the story, but since they had met before, and - after all - Zavis was president, he thought it likely that he could get more action and better information going directly to the top of the publication chain.

The first person to recognize Zavis was the receptionist in the *Zenith Vid* outer office, and within seconds heads were poking around corners and whispers echoed through the section. He was directed through the corridors to the office of Cahill, and he was amused to find the corridor suddenly filled with people taking a break from their business, to get a look at him.

Cahill welcomed Zavis with a handshake and offered him a drink.

"Mr. President," he said, "this is a great honor." He wore a brown leisure suit, not much different than Zavis', and a pair of Lapiz Bear shoes. The shoes had to cost a thousand units, but Zavis knew that Cahill was not showing off. Lapiz Bear shoes were the most comfortable in the Concourse. Zavis had tried a pair on once, and if he had been able to afford them, he would have purchased them.

"The pleasure is mine, Mr. Cahill. I appreciate you seeing me with no notice this way. I'm afraid that a half-hour ago I didn't know myself that I was coming."

"Think nothing of it. It can only be a feather in my cap to have you here. Give me something to talk about this weekend when I brag to my fellow publishers."

"You're hardly in a position that you need to worry about appearances to others in your field, Mr. Cahill. You are the biggest communications company on Teretania. Which makes my visit all the more important --"

"You mean Canthay Chine," Cahill said flatly. Zavis thought his jar must have dropped noticeably because Cahill smiled. He turned his back to Zavis, facing a large wall filled with awards and other mementos of his business empire. "Oh yes, I've known for some time. In fact, more people know than you think, President Zavis. I'll give you credit, though"

"Credit? For what, Mr. Cahill?"

"For either maintaining the loyalty of enough people, or hiding the evidence well enough that those people are afraid to come forward."

"I'm not sure where you get your stories, Mr. Cahill, but Canthay Chine is no more a Hybrid than you or me."

"Please. Mr. Zavis" - he dropped the other man's title completely - "No point in denying it. It will come out in tomorrow's editions of vid, comm, and paper. Mind you, a story this big could appear anywhere and within hours it would be all over the ship, don't you think?"

"I'm sure it would, if such a story were supported with facts."

"Facts are helpful, but not always necessary."

Zavis stood. "Obviously you have something in mind beyond circulation, or you would have printed names already. What do you want from me?"

"From you? I didn't ask you to come here, did I? You came to me. What do *you* want?"

Cahill was right, of course. Zavis said, "I want you to stop printing stories that will only damage the government and upset people needlessly, and I would like the name of your source."

"Sources, Mr. Zavis. Plural. Trust me, you have no idea. And what sort of newsman would I be if I gave out the names of my sources. Then again, since you are here...." Cahill grinned.

"Mr. Cahill," Zavis snapped. "Tell me what you want me to hear, and be done with it!" He thought of Canthay, ridiculed. He thought of his government, destroyed. He thought of the people of Teretania, betrayed and scared of what would come next. He thought of himself.

"I'm not a political man, Zavis. I don't really care who is in power. When Teretania was rebuilt if I wasn't happy with the space and allocations to my business I would happily have gone somewhere else in the galaxy, and done just as well. My loyalties are to Teretania only so far as she serves my needs. That might be foreign thinking to you, but I don't care. I'll be around, somewhere, long after you are nothing but a holobust in the governmental halls. But I don't need upheaval to sell my services. I was asked to spread rumor about the Concourse, then about your office, and ultimately to expose Chine as a Hybrid. I took my money and followed my instructions, but now I see a better opportunity. My source wants your government destroyed, and Chine eliminated. Okay, who cares? But now maybe I can get something from you, something more valuable to me than mere units, all for the simple task of not following through with my plan."

"It's obvious what you want, Cahill," Zavis said coolly, moving toward the door, not out of concern or fear, but to let Cahill know that the conversation was almost over. "I can't offer you the kind of money it would take to satisfy a man like you, since you could buy and sell the physical property of my office six times over. You have money, from whomever your so-called accomplices are. You want power."

"Let's call it subtle influences, Mr. Zavis. I've always been a man behind the scenes, and I'm happy in that role."

"If I could give you that influence, I wouldn't do it - even if you had something I needed, which you don't. But then again, you already knew that. Why make this offer?" He opened the door. Each man stated his case. To remain risked saying something he didn't want to reveal, or hearing something he could not ignore.

Cahill never stopped smiling. "Did you think I would expect you to accept my offer? Not right away, no. But I do know you, Mr. Zavis. You are a man of so-called high ideals, willing to sacrifice yourself for the good of your people. You took on the identity of another man, a man who had been murdered by your enemies, and engaged in an affair with a woman you thought to be his wife, who also turned out to be an alien enemy. You conspired with the Concourse to defy Teretanian law, and risked everything you believed in, stood for, and everything you had, to protect Teretania. I think that once you've thought this through, and remove emotion from the equation, you'll do it again. How will it affect this ship to learn that the government continues to lie, President Zavis?"

If Cahill said anything more, it could not be heard behind the closed door. Two guards from Zavis' office met him in the lobby, and escorted him back toward his own offices. He wasn't required to accompany them, but his trip through this section of the ship had been reckless, and in the calm which followed his confrontation, Zavis was grateful for the protection. His popularity was high, but there were always dangers. He might commit political suicide, but he didn't want to commit actual suicide. The meeting with Cahill hadn't gone badly, and as Zavis reviewed the recording on his wristcomm during the return trip, he felt a slight tinge of hope that this crisis could be averted.

It all depended on Canthay. She had worked hard to retain human form for greater and greater periods of time, and if she could continue to have success, they could prove to anyone on Teretania that she was not a surviving Hybrid. Someone could suggest a genetic test, but that would be unwarranted under Teretania law. What, he wondered, would such a test reveal? If necessary, he would take Canthay away from Teretania, if the issues became too much for her. Or could he abandon his duty to the ship?

Back in his offices Zavis handled minor matters and left again, this time just to the apartment he shared with Canthay. He placed his palm against the sensor and the door opened. The apartment wasn't opulently furnished, but they had little to want. Although the prosperity of Teretanians had increased with the new ship and the new relationship with the Concourse planets, Zavis still felt a twinge of guilt at how easy his life often was. He had more than ample entertainment, food, and some luxuries - perks of the office, most of them, and he understood the need to maintain a certain level of comfort for the head of the government, but he often wondered what it would hurt if privately they lived more modestly.

Light music played in the apartment, and Zavis saw that Canthay's private room was locked. They shared their lives fully, but this one small room remained closed to Zavis. For three years Canthay Chine worked at retaining human form for longer and longer periods, and though she was down to less than an hour of each day where she had to return to her Hybrid form, she still refused to let Zavis see her that way. He understood, and while he said repeatedly that his love would not be affected by the sight of her in that form, he was nonetheless glad that vow had not been put to the test. He looked at the timepiece on his comm and realized that he almost never came home at this time. She didn't want him nearby during her Hybrid moments. He turned to leave.

A terrible scream came from the room. Zavis stood frozen for a second, then leaped toward the door. It wouldn't open. He called her name, but no reply came. He ran to the bedroom, fumbled through the drawer desperately trying to find the master key. In what seemed like ages but was only seconds he found it, and bolted toward the door once more. He called out again, but getting no reply, he took a deep breath and opened the door, knowing that he could be facing Canthay in her Hybrid form.

Canthay lay on the floor just as he had always known her, and he would have been relieved but for the pale look to her face and the unconscious expression of pain. He knelt down and lifted her head. She didn't respond at first, but started to move her lips and eyes slightly. Out of the corner of his eye he saw the same news article which had greeted him that morning.

Her eyes opened, and she tried to mouth words. Zavis told her to be still as he called for help, but she shook her head no and pulled him closer. He heard her whisper.

"I did it. We're safe. I did it."

She fell unconscious again.

CHAPTER TEN
BRYCE SPACE
15:22:22

Once Dunn made the decision to rescue Proxima Ser, his life became expendable. He didn't intend to throw it away, but there remained the possibility that Ser's immunity was unique, and therefore infinitely valuable. What was happening in the Concourse? His message may not have gotten through, but it was too risky to send another, and he could get no reply. The last few days had provided some information, none of it good, and few real answers to his plight.

Not long after he escaped from the planet where Ser was taken, Dunn met Treelistanfortencel -- Dunn merely called him Tree. On a small asteroid where Dunn rested while contemplating his next move, he stumbled – literally – onto Tree, and instantly realized that there were exceptions to the xenophobia which encompassed most of the Bryce. Tree rejected the Bryce way of life – one of fear and loathing for all things not Bryce – and like others who shared his views hid on one of the thousands of small asteroids that accompanied planetary systems. The Bryce didn't actively seek out these renegades, but if found, Tree risked being killed.

The asteroid on which they hid was barely large enough to sustain gravity, and Tree half-joked that if he weren't so old he might be able to jump right off into space. Though the rock had a breathable atmosphere it only remained stable a few meters from the ground, after which it became too thin for life. Tree remained in the feeble valleys, where he was not

119

only hidden but where the concentration of oxygen would keep him alive. Dunn realized that the Bryce were fearful – and homicidal – toward not only other races, but even toward their own. Dunn struggled to understand that point of view. After all, weren't all people – all creatures – born however they were? Weren't there good and bad in all races and species? He'd learned that even the Gorups and the Brodians had those who didn't hate humans – and, now he knew, so did the Bryce. He and Ser had argued the point many times in the early days of their mission, before they'd realized the futility of trying to find common ground.

Dunn's ship was able to sustain him for a while, and could recharge his oxygen tanks almost indefinitely – but time remained a serious issue. Ser needed help immediately, and the Bryce remained a threat, so any rescue mission had to take place immediately. Tree offered the use of his vessel, small and slow though it was. Dunn considered the options – with Tree's vessel he could possibly get closer to Ser, but it would strand Tree on the asteroid, and it would deprive Dunn of the uncontaminated oxygen he needed. Despite the dangers of using his own ship, that was the only choice.

Dunn left the asteroid, and armed with the slight information Tree had been able to provide, headed for the Bryce homeworld. The buffer zone of uninhabited planets and strength of the Bryce Effect, ironically, gave the xenophobic race a sense of security on their homeworld. Although large vessels would be unable to penetrate the defenses undetected, a small ship with power down and all weapons inactive, could sneak through. It was a high risk gamble, but worth taking. Dunn spent the half-day of travel to the Bryce world trying to rest, trying to summon whatever strength and courage he had for what he knew could be his last day. The slightest rupture of his suit, the slightest hint of detection, and he would be dead. Buoyed by the knowledge that he had no real course open but the one he was taking, Dunn felt a sense of calm.

As he approached the planet Dunn noted how few ships his sensors could detect. Granted, powered down his sensors were passive-only, but he still anticipated more ship traffic in the upper atmosphere. The Bryce had the technology, though perhaps not on the scale of the Concourse. Or was he guessing? Then again, what would a race that wants no contact care about space travel? There would be little exploration, little need for it other than as protection.

Tree suggested that Ser might be kept in what he called the *Apathorium*, the primary laboratory where the Bryce Effect was created and where other species were tested. When Dunn asked him to define tested, Tree refused – but that was answer enough.

Stealth was useless, and hoping to be unnoticed was equally pointless. This mission would be bold, all-or-nothing, and anything but subtle. He chose the Bryce night for his attempt, though he didn't know whether in this place that would be an advantage.

As he burned his way through the atmosphere Dunn readied himself.

Bryce and humans, to his sensors, were almost identical. The Bryce were slightly smaller and thinner on average, based on the few he'd seen in reports and during the mission, but they would blend very easily in human society. This made Dunn shiver, because he thought the Bryce, should they decide to attack the Concourse, could do it rather effectively.

It would be impossible to find a single human among the Bryce using his ship's sensors, except that he knew the specifics of Proxima Ser's body signature – a necessary part of working on any mission. It would be difficult, but within a kilometer he might be able to find her signal. A kilometer was very little time to do what he had in mind.

He successfully penetrated the outer atmosphere and moved beneath the cloud cover. If spotted now he would be recognized as alien immediately, but there was no time to consider that. There were ships on the outer ranges of his sensors – which likely meant that he could be on theirs – but he pushed it to the back of his mind and sped toward the building where Ser might be – if she wasn't, the mission was over.

The structure described by Tree stood at least a dozen stories tall, which was more than double any others around, or any he had seen on the other world. He moved his sensors into active mode and placed his ship in a holding pattern above the building. Probably visible from the ground, and certainly moving in an unusual manner, Dunn ignored his vulnerability and studied the screen while his heart rate raced and his body temperature soared.

There! He found what looked like Proxima Ser's body signature, on the seventh level, roughly 40 meters inside the walls. Good, he thought, she's not too close to the outer walls. He took manual control of the ship and swept down toward her prison. His ship moved well – the choice of a small, fast, maneuverable ship was a good one. He stopped just outside the walls at the seventh level, and activated his weapons. Holding his breath for a moment to steady himself, Dunn fired. The laser hit the walls and immediately they started to crumble and burn. He wanted to breach the walls, but not too deeply, lest he hurt Ser or ruin any chance of getting out once he found her. He swept the guns across the surrounding area, not so much to destroy as to stun and scare anyone who might still be there. Already in his protective suit, Dunn moved the ship almost directly against the gaping hole, placed it in a hovering position, ran to the airlock and – careful to seal the inner lock first – opened the outer seal and jumped into the building.

He hit hard, and the floor beneath him started to crumble. Gathering his energy, Dunn ran forward and a little to the left to avoid the collapse. Getting back, he knew, would be tough. He had no ability to detect Ser with his suit, so relied merely on where the ship said she might be. He moved forward past two bodies and into a corridor that went both left and right. There were doors on either side of him, but likely only one would contain Ser. There was no way to know, so he guessed left and moved that way quickly, blasting the door open with his pistol.

The room inside had crumbled, and dust filled the air. Dunn couldn't see anything, and his visor filters didn't help much. He stood, hoping the dust would settle, and as it did his heart sank. In the corner of the room, lying strapped to a table, connected to dozens of tubes and wires, with a pile of rubble covering her bloodied body, was Proxima Ser.

Around her three Bryce lay, one woman still struggling for life. Dunn blasted her.

The rubble over Ser was solid, but not heavy, for which Dunn was grateful – a metal/resin combination that he didn't take time to view closely. He tossed away the largest pieces, aware that his rescue attempt could have killed Ser, and equally aware that every minute that passed would bring Bryce closer to his position. He saw no movement from Ser, but ignored that for the moment, pulling out wires and tubes as quickly yet as delicately as time would allow. Sounds from the distance – outside the building, he guessed – became louder, so he picked her up, tossed her over his shoulder, and moved from the room. The dust continued to interfere with his sight, and the limited peripheral vision his visor allowed, combined with the body of Ser cover one side, made him wary of every step – weak flooring or falling rubble could end the mission, and their lives, as quickly as a Bryce blaster.

His ship came into view, but damage to the structure made a direct route impossible. He slid to his right, his back to the wall, and moved along the outside of the room, balancing Ser, hoping the edges of the floor wouldn't give way. He couldn't see his feet, and dared not look down to focus on them. The sounds outside were much louder, and glancing to his right he saw blasts hit his ship – small spears of light, most likely hand-held weapons. The ship lurched slightly with each hit, and Dunn knew that the wrong location, the lucky hit for a Bryce, would take it down.

Movement to his left came swiftly – an arm grabbed at his suit, momentarily seizing it. Dunn pulled his arm free, and the momentum carried them away from the wall. Off balance and with the weight of Ser pulling them toward the gulf below, Dunn grabbed a pipe with his free hand just in time. He steadied them, but saw the arm coming toward him again as the Bryce who had followed him along the wall made another attempt. Two others stood at the doorway, ready but unable to assist on the narrow walkway. The floor beneath cracked. There was no time to fight, and no chance of success. Dunn continued to move along the wall, as close to a run as he could, and as he stayed just a step ahead of the man pursuing him, he stomped with his foot at the weakened metal/resin floorboard behind him. The pursuer grabbed at him again, just as the floor crumbled. His fingers gripped Dunn's suit, then as the floor disappeared beneath the man he held on – for his life – but gravity pulled him down and he disappeared with a scream in the dust and rubble below. Dunn had almost reached the hole in the outer wall be had blasted, but there were no stirrings from Ser, and he could see a small hole in his suit where the hand ripped it before falling away.

He reached the opening. The outer hatchway was open and he tossed Ser in, unable to be gentle. A beam bounced off the wall beside him, and others followed. At least a dozen Bryce were firing from below, most at the ship, but some had noticed Dunn and were training their guns on him. Dunn jumped into the airlock falling and stumbling, cautious not to land on Ser in case she still lived. He rose and hit the control to seal the doorway.

A moment of decision came. The time to excise the air from the chamber and refill it from inside would be too long. By then the Bryce would have disabled the ship - if they hadn't already accomplished that. Besides, the hole in his suit may have already doomed him, so Dunn opened the inner lock and stumbled toward the pilot's chair. His ship was pre-programmed for quick escape, so it took just three seconds to set it in motion and start the ascent. Blaster scars on the transparent shield showed him that the ship had sustained many blasts, but the strength was relatively weak. Hopefully the ship would function.

They climbed quickly into the atmosphere. He couldn't engage full engines until they were in space – the drag of the air around them would create too much friction, burn them up. He needed to climb into, but the solid fuel was already critically low. A couple miles separated them from the freedom of space, where fuel meant little to these engines – but here, in the atmosphere, it meant everything. Dunn looked for pursuers, but none came – yet. He closed the airlock with Ser inside, then proceeded to empty the air from the interior of the ship, resupply it from his reserves. That done, and now almost out of the planet's atmosphere, he opened the airlock once again. There was no way to completely purge the airlock of Bryce contaminates without killing Ser, but he hoped that the concentration of whatever could kill had been lessened by mixing with the ship's air when he first stepped in, and whatever remained might not be fatal. He looked at his suit and the rip, about 2 cm wide. The exchange of air as complete as possible, he pulled off the top of his suit and bent over Proxima Ser, finally able to see if she was still alive.

In the silence and stillness of the ship he watched. She was breathing! Faintly, shallow, and not without difficulty, but she was breathing. Dunn placed his arms under her shoulders to lift her. He'd take her inside, check her injuries, and do what he could.

A wave of nausea poured over him. The room turned, he saw a blue haze form over his eyes, and as the Bryce Effect took hold Dunn hoped that if Ser could live and get them back, she would see that he was buried at the family plot on Earth.

CHAPTER ELEVEN
PLANET IDONA
15:22:22

Caleb Alletson woke up in the middle of the night, as planned. His parents slept on the floor above, and he'd readied himself for this night for a long time; it was surprising he'd slept at all. His brother stirred in his bed in the room they shared but didn't awaken. He watched his brother, Garl, age five, sleep. He slept more soundly than normal, his stomach fuller than it had been in a while. Caleb had given Garl his ration that night, telling him that he wasn't hungry, that he'd found some fruit in town earlier in the day and couldn't eat another bite. In truth, Caleb was very hungry, but if he could complete his task tonight that wouldn't be a problem, for him or for his family.

The Bryce War hit them hard, as Caleb supposed it always did the economically lower class families. On the news they always called it "middle class" but he didn't see where there was any middle to it at all. Those with more money – some had a little more, some a lot more, and some indescribably more – seemed to be just fine, and those who had nothing always seemed to be the first to get help from the government and private organizations. His family – mother, father, his two sisters and his brother Garl - didn't qualify for the programs, but didn't seem to have enough to afford anything but the most basic foods. The farm had long since turned to dust, and his father tried everything else that could be tried – with little success before the war, but none once it started.

Rationing – he'd come to hate the word – had been forced on most of the planet because of the attacks. Ships couldn't get through often enough from the supplier planets; the number of Bryce infiltrators was just enough to keep panic among the markets. Food was scarce, and prices were crazy. The government prevented gouging on some necessities, but not enough, and they couldn't insure that local officials handled it properly. The Alletsons struggled to get by on a few pounds of grains, some fruits, rare vegetables – he hadn't tasted meat in months.

But Caleb could change that.

He slipped out the door and down the hall. His sisters, twins and just a couple years younger than Caleb, slept peacefully. He stopped briefly to say a quiet goodbye, then headed outside, already dressed, rearming the security system, and moving quickly down the road.

On his sixteenth birthday a week before his mother had baked him a cake – using almost two days worth of rations for the party. He appreciated the gesture his parents made, wanting to show him some of the normalcy that had been his life before the war. But the consumption of such valuable rations for him, for a day that would come year after year, pushed him to find a solution, and one of his friends, Berry, had hinted what that might be.

"As soon as I am sixteen, I'm joining the Concourse Defense Force," he had said.

"The CDF?" Caleb replied. "Why? I mean, if you want to go into the service, just join the Idonian army or something like that – why get directly involved in the battles with the Bryce? I'm for unity and all that, but without a degree where can you go in the CDF? You need at least a minor degree to get into any officer training – heck, that's two years, minimum."

His friend looked around as though he had just committed a crime or had a special secret. "I'll join on the Temporary Enlistment Bill. Once the war is over, I come home. In the meantime I get meals, I get health care, and I make enough money to fight off some of this wretched rationing for my family."

Caleb had heard all this of course, except the last. "What can you do about rationing, if you're light years away? You don't make enough money, even on the TE Bill, to pay these black market prices."

His friend looked around again. "You can if you join Advance Patrol."

They laughed it off, but the thought stayed in Caleb's mind. Advanced Patrol – the first line against the Bryce, the men who seek them out, who volunteer to venture into known Bryce-infested zones, and who sometimes have to do it without suit protection. They weren't the strongest or the best trained fighters, but they were the bravest of the CDF.

Or, he thought, the most desperate.

Caleb reached the CDF Recruitment Center; it was 4 a.m. He was surprised to find that he wasn't there alone, and had to wait to speak with one of the agents. After a short wait, as he wondered what his parents would think when they woke up to find his empty bed, a tall, thin man introduced himself. Caleb explained that he wanted to join the CDF, and produced the documents and ID cards which showed he was now of age to make that decision.

"You want to join under the TE Bill?" the man confirmed. "You understand that while you'll be released once the Bryce threat is over, there's no telling when that will be. You can't believe what you hear on the news about progress and new breakthroughs to the Bryce Effect and all that. We're honest with you here – we don't know if you're talking about weeks, months, years, or whatever." The man – from Izar, Caleb supposed – looked at him with a grim expression. Caleb didn't pay much attention to the news. He knew the war was going badly. He knew that things would get worse before they got better, and that while he had confidence in the Concourse's ability to defeat the Bryce – after all, they'd beaten the Brodians, the Gorups, the Hybrids, and Vandettri – it wouldn't be easy, and the cost would be high. He'd considered joining anyway, but now he had no choice.

"Yes, sir," he replied. "I understand this is open-ended."

"You're too young to be an officer, so you realize that without any special training you'll have limited options, that your tasks will be lower level, your danger level a little higher."

"I want Advance Patrol."

With that the man stiffened. The AP sustained the highest casualty rate of any in the war. Fully 10% of the men in the AP had been killed in the last few months. Many accepted the job, but he hadn't had anyone come looking for it. He was about to ask the boy why he wanted to do it when Caleb said:

"The pay's a lot better, right? I can have it sent directly to my family here, can't I?"

The man pursed his lips, nodded slowly. As he processed the young boy, in a matter of minutes changing him from poor farmer's son into a soldier of the CDF, a member of the Advance Patrol, he looked at him with admiration, and at this situation with shame. When men and boys came to him to join because they had a need to serve, when they came because their lives were messed up too much to stay, when they came looking for a future, he saw purpose in his work. Today, as Caleb signed the papers for no other reason than he saw it as the only way to feed his family, the man cried a little.

***

CONCOURSE HEADQUARTERS
MEETING ROOM OF THE WAR COMMITTEE
15:22:23

Eight men and women sat in the room. One, Charles Forrester, sat alone facing the other seven. In the weeks since the Committee on the Conduct of the War had been created their power had increased dramatically. Forrester hadn't supported their creation, but tolerated it, and this had proven to be a big mistake.

The seven "judges" (that was, Forrester thought, the role they have claimed) sat side-by-side on a bench fully three feet higher than the floor, three feet higher than Forrester, who stood behind an empty table. Behind Forrester was a gallery, enough seating for a hundred people, all empty – for the moment. The room had been designed and constructed as a courtroom, and whether they legally had the power or not to conduct trials, there was no doubt that soon they would be doing just that.

The War Committee members were: Merwa Yon; Ambassador Venge of Complet; Ambassador

Enoi of Alleghany; Ambassador Henderson of Earth; Ambassador Kline of Renna; Dr. Lortinne, a psychologist, also from Earth; and Armab-Holt, a military scientist from Melanin. The only one who Forrester thought might support him in any way was Enoi, and the recent devastation of Alleghany had weakened his resolve and support considerably.

"I only have ten minutes, gentlemen," Forrester started, "so forgive me if I am brief with my report." He continued to speak respectfully and cooperatively with the committee, although they seldom did the same.

Kline, the Rennite, who was spokesman for the committee most often, said, "Mr. Forrester, we will need more of your time on daily basis if we're to have all the information we need to conduct the war."

Forrester looked directly at Kline. "Ambassador Kline, this committee doesn't conduct the war. The council to which you report, and by whose devices you exist, does not conduct this war. Whether you prefer to accept it or not, the Concourse, of which I am Director and military head, conducts this war. I have agreed to meet with you on a daily basis, even though I find it a non-productive use of my time, but I cannot spare a long time for this. Besides, you send me twenty written requests for information every day, to which I reply, and I personally speak with most of you almost every day."

"Yes, but the information you provide is not complete." Kline looked down at the papers in front of him. "In the medical laboratories there recently was a theory proposed of a DNA mutation which might – the operative word here is might – have some impact on the Bryce Effect. You've given permission to pursue this most extreme method of research, and in fact it has been going on for quite a while, but you've not informed the committee, so we can report to the Concourse Council—"

Merwa Yon interrupted. "These are not the Battle of Teretania days, Forrester. You don't have free reign to do whatever you please, use whatever excuse you choose for your plans, and expect that no one will discover them."

Forrester didn't look at Yon, but kept his gaze squarely on Kline. "Ambassador Kline, it's not my intention, nor my responsibility, to inform this Committee of every step we take. To suggest that I do would be to completely destroy my effectiveness as Commander-in-Chief of the Concourse Defense Forces. A certain amount of secrecy must be maintained in military matters – and in this case medical matters are military in nature. Some of you –" he looked at Armab-Holt, but not at Yon – "have military backgrounds, and know that full disclosure is not only impossible, it is irresponsible. The studies you speak of, theoretical in nature, are part of that military strategy. If there's something substantive that I need to report I will inform the council, through this body if they choose. However, there seems to be little need, since by questioning every move made by most every member of the Concourse, in addition to creating at atmosphere of hostility and paranoia, you appear to get your information readily enough."

Kline ignored the last comment and said, "I also see that you've removed one of your cabinet members, Horace Keweenaw, Secretary of Education. This is quite an extreme move to make at any time, and we feel –" he swept his hand across the bench to indicate everyone, some of who nodded – "that we should have been given the chance to inform the council of your intention, and that they might have the need to approve of your decision, since it was the council, after all, who approved his appointment."

"They confirmed it," Forrester said, "and they will have the opportunity to confirm my next selection, but it was my choice to hire him, and I can fire him if I see fit. That decision, even if the council had the authority to approve the removal of an office-holder, lies far outside the jurisdiction of your committee, even with the extreme latitude the council sees fit to provide you. I don't need to answer for personal matters, even less than for military matters."

"The council may not agree."

"The council can remove me at their whim," Forrester said. "That has always been their power. I wonder what the people of the Concourse, however, would think of such an act. We may be at war, and this body might be working vigorously to place the blame at my office and to grab for itself any power it can, but unless or until the council decides to remove me, I will conduct my office as I see fit. Ten minutes has passed, by my reckoning, so I must return to my official duties." He turned to leave.

Merwa Yon said, "I find it offensive that you didn't reply to me, Forrester. I think you show a lack of respect for the authority of this body."

Now Forrester stopped and looked directly at Merwa Yon. "The authority of this body, by law, is the authority to ask questions and report to the council. Within the framework of that limitation, I respect it enough to take time out from my conduct of the war to speak with this body. Whether or not I respect individual members is without value – and where respect is not offered, it will not be returned. The traditional address to the Director of the Concourse is Mr. Forrester or Mr. Director. Furthermore, for the duration of the war, if this body wants daily reports, it can make an appointment with my office. I don't have time to come into this private trial forum when there are more pressing matters."

With that Forrester left the room. His anger was real, his indignation sincere, but some of his venom was used as a smokescreen. While they argued about his impertinence and jostled with whether they should try to force their views on him further, he had to repair the leak in his medical research – as he had done in his cabinet by getting rid of Horace Keweenaw, the War Committee spy.

***

"What happened, Cahill?"

No longer a member of the Concourse government and able to flout his private power, Merwa Yon didn't need to meet in secret anymore. His latest meeting with Cahill took place in the vidman's office, visible though not audible to anyone who happened by.

"What happened is that we had the perfect set-up to expose Chine as a Hybrid, and she found a way to stop us." Cahill, threw his hands up in an expression of surprise and surrender. "We invited her to the rally – a rally we designed, we supported, we paid for and we had ready to use to out advantage – and she accepted readily enough. There was no way she could stay longer than a couple hours without turning into her Hybrid form – we know that from history, Yon – and we had the exits rigged to break down when she tried to leave."

"So – what went wrong?"

"She didn't leave! For seven hours, maybe longer, she stayed right there in the public eye, on camera, talking, interacting, looking and sounding completely human."

"That's not possible. I read the official reports, not just that media crap, and I ran the Hybrid prisons. I know she couldn't have done that if she is a Hybrid."

"Well, she did it. Either she's not a Hybrid and you've been wrong all along, or she's found a way to get around the three-hour limit."

"Or she's an imposter," Yon said.

"Doesn't matter. If she's an imposter – which I seriously doubt, because to everyone there, including me, that was Chine – then there's no point in trying to expose a human as a Hybrid, and even if she is a Hybrid, with that seven-hour exposure as evidence, there's an automatic defense to any accusations we make, now. Overt or direct, all anyone has to say is, 'Look – there she is – you had her on your camera for seven hours and she's completely human.' I don't know what happened, but we've killed our own plan."

Yon walked out of the office quickly. "Killed, yes – but not my plan."

CHAPTER TWELVE
BRYCE SPACE
15:22:23

The first thing he noticed was pain, and a blue haze that covered his mind, even with his eyes closed. Dunn opened his eyes, and though the blue hue remained he was undoubtedly alive and in the ship. He lay in his bunk. An intravenous drip poised above him and as consciousness became the norm he looked around. The ship was traveling in deep space, and Proxima Ser sat in the pilot's seat, looking at him. She looked weak, beaten, and pale – but she looked determined and Dunn could see that, unless there was something he was missing, she would be okay.

"What the Hell did you do?" She commanded.

"It's good to see you, too," he quipped.

"Seriously, Dunn – just what did you do? We're heading back to the Concourse, and until a few minutes ago had dozens of Bryce ships in pursuit. We outran them, but it was close. You disobeyed orders and came after me?"

"Yes, I disobeyed orders. Look, Proxima – orders are designed for the expected events – this was different. You have immunity, and maybe no one else does – that alone made it necessary to come after you. You shouldn't have even been on this mission because of your immunity – sure, it might have kept you alive when they caught you, but for that same reason you might be too valuable to have risked. I disobeyed orders – you want to report me when we get back, great - but wait until we get back."

She managed a smile. "Well. After you dropped the building on me I don't recall anything until I woke up and found you dying. You saved my life, I managed to save yours – I guess we can forget your crime for now. I don't know how you got me out, but that had to be one heck of a task."

Dunn looked again at the IV above him. "It was interesting – not something that they taught me at the academy, I'll tell you that. But I don't get it – how did you save me? Did you find a cure to the Bryce Effect?"

"Not really – not a cure, although I learned a lot while I was in their hands. They never bothered to mask their their actions, since they never expected that I would ever get out of there alive. But as for you, the exposure was limited, but I think you would have died in a short time if I hadn't come to. I took a chance that whatever I have in me could help you, so I gave you a transfusion. Not much – after what happened I gathered I didn't have much to give. But since your exposure was slight it seems to have done the trick."

"Am I out of danger?"

"As far as I know. Look, this is all guesswork. If the Bryce Effect comes back on you I don't think I can help. I can't spare the blood and we don't have the facilities here to replicate it. We're still a few days from Concourse space, so if the treatment is temporary I'm out of options for you, so let's just cross our fingers."

"Thanks."

"You did the same for me – though I don't know how I am going to report this once we arrive."

"No need to bother your conscience. I sent a message when you were captured, so my court martial won't be at the expense of your conscience – but that's not what matters right now. What did you find out?"

A lot of it is guesswork, and I don't know how much I can trust my memory," she said, stifling a cough between her words. "The Bryce Effect is something they created, a DNA mutation that is now inherent in most born Bryce. Not all, from what I could tell, but a vast majority. Thing is, my immunity is chemical in nature – I have a chemical in my body that blocks the effect. And, despite your heroics, I doubt that I am unique. Unusual maybe, but the chemical matrix I observed isn't impossible to find in humanoid races, to varying degrees. I studied biochemistry before the CDF training, so I was familiar with some of what I heard. I wrote it down before it left my mind, while I was waiting to see what happened with you."

Pain shot through Dunn's body – whether it was a return of the Bryce effect or simply leftovers from the efforts to get to Ser he couldn't say. It appeared that his fate was pretty much out of his own control, so he pushed concern to the back of his mind. "It appears that between the two of us we learned a lot. You know what makes them dangerous, and I learned a little about what makes them tick."

She nodded. "I started to read your report, but it's a bit early for me to focus on anything too long. So, you befriended one of them. A stroke of luck, I'd say."

"Yeah – and it's interesting what they believe. They see themselves as the chosen people, that they will one day inherit the galaxy through some mythical difference between their race and the other humanoid races in this part of the universe. Seems to me that except for the paranoia, they're pretty much like everyone else. They could live, work, and probably interbreed with other Concourse peop---"

Ser stood up suddenly, her face a twisted expression of disgust. "Don't say things like that." She started to walk away.

Dunn called after her. "Hey, I'm sorry. What did I say? They're enemies right now, but that doesn't mean they can't ultimately be friends."

"Look, I don't mind being peaceful, and I don't mind being friends, but to suggest that planets should start interbreeding – that's just sick."

"Ser, planets have been interbreeding for a couple centuries."

"Well, they shouldn't. Equality is a great theory, but the simple fact is, some humanoid races are better than others – and it doesn't make any sense for any of them to mix. We can get along, but we're not the same." Her face showed a sourness that Dunn hadn't seen before. True, she had never been overly friendly, and they hadn't exactly become close during their mission, but he didn't realize she was a planetary racist – and it made little sense to find that in someone so closely aligned with the CDF.

"Whoa, I'm sorry. I never thought it was a sore spot. Hey, look at us – we're from places hundreds of light years apart, but look what it took to save my life, a little bit of ---"

"That's different – and I'm not altogether sure that it's something that should normally happen. Look, I have nothing against you, or your people, but when you suggest that yours and mine, and things like the Bryce, should interbreed, making some happy and gray homogeneous galaxy, it's more than I care to discuss. I have to say, although their methods are wrong, I'm not completely unsympathetic to the idea behind the Bryce isolationism. I mean, how much better would we be if everyone just kept to themselves? A lot, I think."

The conversation slowed after that. Dunn fell back to sleep, Ser worked on remembering her observations and trying to get a message ready to send to the Concourse. But to whom should she send it? Her duty said she must report to Forrester, but something told her that Merwa Yon, the Chief of Intelligence, understood the situation better. Getting the message through was the easy part – figuring out where it should go kept her thinking for hours.

CHAPTER THIRTEEN
CONCOURSE HEADQUARTERS
15:22:25

The two men didn't know each other, had never met, and in all likelihood would never run into each other again. They both preferred it that way. They passed in the corridor at the designated time each wearing the correct colors, carrying the correct material, and passing it between them quickly and without any words. As they each moved along they completed a new phase in the battle against the Bryce Effect.

One of the men, General Monroc, felt the module in his hands and felt the beads of sweat form on his brow. The War Committee was everywhere now, and their power continued to grow. Suddenly the council seemed unable or unwilling to act without approval of the committee. Monroc didn't understand it – the council appeared subservient to the War Committee – or at least so trusting that it didn't questions anything coming from it.

Recently Forrester told him of the committee's determination to follow every facet of the war, including the medical experiments. They tried to keep information away from them, but that was becoming more and more difficult. It was Monroc who suggested that they duplicate everything being studied, in a military lab hidden away on the other side of Teretania. Forrester resisted, and Monroc understood why – it meant once again turning to subterfuge and secrecy to accomplish the goals, something he supposed Forrester had decided never to do again.

But this committee – what they could observe they tried to control, directly or indirectly. Already influential people who had fought against their influence found themselves terminated from projects, and a few had even been arrested on vague suspicions of even more vague charges. Though the charges most likely would never hold up in court, they had the effect of getting a foe out of the way and of eliminating that person's power for the time being, if not forever.

Monroc was a fighter – one of the few, he supposed, who held any sway these days. Patriotism was high, but true fighters were still hard to come by. He fought Forrester in the early days of the war, pushed for greater action, faster action, and more forceful action. He still thought Forrester was wrong about a lot of the strategies he chose – but that didn't matter. Forrester was commander, and Monroc was duty-bound to follow his orders, and to protect his interests as long as they remained with the letter of the law.

It took an hour to reach the lab, and another ten minutes of checking documents and making sure no one followed him before he could enter the main laboratory. Dr. Stapleton waited for him and held out his hand the minute the general arrived.

"It would be much better if I could talk with the other researchers, General," he said.

"No doubt, doctor – but they can't testify that they've shared information with you if they don't know about it. Most of this is compiled by one person, someone willing to risk his career and perhaps his life and freedom by recording this data. We dare not involve others."

The doctor placed the hydrantium data module into the reader. The clear glass tube, no more than a couple inches long and half an inch wide, contained a chemical unit which had become the most efficient means of data storage and sharing. Barring the fracture of the casing itself, something which would take more effort than one man could manage, the data was secure. "All I am saying is that I could do better with better data. I know you politician's have your reasons."

Monroc's blood boiled at the thought. "I'm not a politician, doctor. I am a military man, and we follow orders. I've explained to you the reason behind them because I respect you, but if I didn't know them, I would still do the same thing."

"Hmmm hmmm," the doctor said, now half listening. He studied the readout on the screen – the accumulation of the survivor studies, experiments in chemical compounds, physical barriers, and most recently DNA mutations. This was what he was looking for.

"Well, General Monroc, even though you don't take orders from me, I think you'd be well served to get Charles Forrester down here as soon as possible. If they are half as good as me over at the other lab – and I suspect they are – you're probably only a day or two away from finding a cure to the Bryce Effect."

***

Forrester requested a meeting with the Concourse Council for the next day. He received a notice an hour later that he was to appear before the War Committee, a full hour before he planned to meet with the council. Technically, refusing the subpoena could make him subject to arrest, but he gambled that even with their increased power the committee wouldn't dare such a move. To make sure, though, Forrester announced throughout the media that he planned to met with the council, and that the matters were critical to the quick end of the war. He hoped it might be true, but whether it really was or not wasn't the most important thing – if the committee tried to stop him now they would be perceived as hampering the war effort, perhaps of trying to do so for their own purposes, and their power might be destroyed. It was a gamble he felt confident he could take – but not one he would press too often.

The council chambers stood full with members, media, and hundreds of spectators standing in the aisles and outer corridors. The vid cameras stood ready, and whatever was to pass had the earmarks of an historic event – and Forrester didn't want that.

"Mr. President," he addressed the head of the council, "I requested this meeting to discuss urgent matters, but a public forum is not the best place to have such a discussion. I respectfully request that we adjourn to a private setting." He could hear the murmurs of the crowd; it was risky, to suggest openly that he wanted to keep information from the people, but as he watched the war go badly and his own political power wane, he was taking greater and greater risks on both fronts.

"Mr. Director. If you had wished a private meeting, the Committee on the Conduct of the War would have been happy to accommodate you in that manner. It is the policy of this body that no meeting be conducted in secret. We're public servants – as you are – and to meet clandestinely would be a violation of our charter. The Committee was designed to be our eyes and ears. My understanding is that you were requested to appear before them earlier today, but declined. It would be wrong to accommodate you in that manner."

"Councilmen – respectfully. You have chosen to trust eyes which only let you see what they wish you to see, and ears which only let you hear what they choose for you to hear. How many of you are present when the War Committee conducts its questioning? Outside the committee membership, do you know the powers they have assumed for themselves? They purport to be an extension of you, but they do more than investigate. They obstruct, they interrogate, they interfere with the conduct not only of the war, but of more Concourse business than you have ever felt it necessary to become involved with."

"Are you concerned that they threaten your power, Mr. Forrester?"

Although he had suspected for a while, the direction of the events that morning gave Forrester clarity in what had happened. The council, through the War Committee, had been able to do an end-around the popular vote, around the will of the majority of the people. By creating an "observing" body and allowing that body, independent of the council, to battle the executive office, without directly confronting Forrester and his office about matters, the council could stay protected from any public backlash. If Forrester failed, *he* would fall. If the committee failed, it might fall but the council would be spared. Yes, they sought to remove Forrester's power – and it was working – without risking their own. But now wasn't the time to confront that issue.

"I'm not concerned about the power or responsibilities of my office," Forrester said, "except where it concerns victory in the war against the Bryce. The information I have, which I am duty bound to present before the council – not legally, but ethically bound – is such that to present it in an open forum would compromise its value."

"Then I repeat myself, Mr. Forrester – why not present it to the committee? They will make a recommendation on your proposal and the council can vote one way or another."

"Then, Mr. President and members of the council, I submit to you that for me to meet with the committee is unnecessary. They already have all the information I would bring to you. In fact, what I planned to bring to you today they have known for almost a full day. No, I didn't meet with them, but they have operators in many sectors of the Concourse government. The committee has been more than your eyes and ears, ladies and gentlemen – it has operated as your brain, and your conscience. To appear before the committee would be waste of my time, and any recommendation they chose to make to this body they would have already made – if they wanted you to have the information. Obviously, they do not."

The council erupted in multiple discussions. The member of the Committee, four of whom sat on the council at first were struck dumb, but protested most loudly when they realized the effect of Forrester's words.

The council President pounded his gavel. "Order! Order! Mr. Director – "

Ambassador Venge of Complet, member of the War Committee, stood and – in a breach of strict council procedure – spoke over the President. "Director Forrester, such accusation is dangerous, and could very well lead to a new vote for your removal."

Forrester smiled slightly. Perhaps that's exactly what was needed. "Perhaps it could. Allow me to make statement, then, which might clear this up more quickly." He turned toward the cameras and crowd more than to the council. "I have come today because we have made a discovery which could quickly and completely end the war with the Bryce. The War Committee, whose authority is not recognized by the Concourse charter, nor was ever voted or approved by the people, has this information but has not shared it with the council. I want to share it with the council, but would you have me present it here, where anyone sympathetic to or in league with the Bryce could pass that information along quickly and easily making it useless? Will we allow thousands or millions more to die because one small committee is brokering for power or because the council, mindful of the secrecy that was necessary in the past, will make a mistake that is opposite but no less fatal?

I am Commander of the Concourse Defense Force. I can take the steps necessary to win this war without approval from the council or any *ad hoc* committee. I came here today because I, too mindful of the secrecy of the past more so than anyone else here, want my actions to be approved by the council, if at all possible. If the council will not meet with me and cooperate in this matter, I will take the steps I need to take. They can choose to remove me, but that requires a vote to conduct a hearing, and two days notice, by which time either the war will be won or lost."

The Concourse Council immediately adjourned to meet with Forrester privately.

***

Away from the formality of a public event, Forrester simply talked.

"Here's what we know: The Bryce Effect is something which is structured into their DNA. Once we learned that, we searched for a genetic answer, and think we've found it. The survivors of Bryce attacks all share a common genetic trait, one which seems to be brought about either through interplanetary lineage or significant racial mixture within a planet's gene pool."

"The mixing of people from various planets is a recent humanoid phenomenon, not common, and still discouraged in many societies, so this trait is much rarer. More common is that person within a planet whose parents, grandparents, and ancestors back many generations, encountered more races, and interbred between them. Outside of this trait we can find no commonality which would explain immunity to the Bryce Effect. The only immediate action we have taken is to change the personnel involved in Advance Patrol. Knowing that those with a greater racial mix are more likely to be immune, we have rotated soldiers so those who do not have that trait aren't put in any greater danger than is necessary. This doesn't insure any more protection for those who have the trait, and they are not as yet aware of that protection, but we think it is a good first step."

Forrester punched buttons in front of him, and immediately information appeared on a screen in front of each of the council members. Forrester watched the Committee members to see if he could detect any signs that they had seen this before – he knew they had, because his spies knew who their spies were, thought he hoped their spies didn't know who his spies were – but he was unable to see a difference.

"Our geneticists have devised a DNA mutation, one which we have every reason to believe will counteract the Bryce Effect."

The council stirred. The president said, "A mutation? You're suggesting that we subject ourselves to a mutation? I can tell you right now, Mr. Forrester, that this solution is unacceptable. Can you predict what the effects will be?"

"I understand that this is an extreme solution – and this is why I needed to bring it before the council. More than perhaps at any time in its existence, the council holds the future of the humanoid race in its hands – and the decision is difficult. Yes, we have tested it, though only for a very short period of time, under very controlled circumstances."

Another council member interrupted. "Are you saying that you actually used this – this genetic disfigurement – on people? You did this to them?"

"Yes, we did. We used volunteers only, those who we knew did not have any multi-racial lineage. We gave them the mutation, and we exposed them to the Bryce Effect. Although we've had only 25 hours of testing, the results have been successful. One solider – Caleb Alletson from Idona – was exposed to a full force Bryce Effect, and has suffered no ill effects at all."

"And if he should die tomorrow – if he should become disfigured or carry something fatal to the next generation? What good will your solution be then, Mr. Director?"

"I agree it is a scary possibility, but our scientists think that it is a benign mutation. There are no total guarantees, but the alternative is to continue to face the Bryce – something we cannot do without losing in the end. They have greater resources than we ever expected, a stronger willingness to sacrifice thousands if not millions, we are receiving no help from other empires, federations or people, and our strength, still weakened because of the Battle of Teretania and the war before that, simply cannot stand the continued assault. We are losing, and my intelligence suggests that the Bryce have a large attack coming – something greater than all the other attacks put together, something that will decimate the humanoid people and perhaps extinguish it."

***

In his office two hours later, General Monroc, Doctor Stapleton, and Charles Forrester met. Forrester placed armed guards at all the entrances to the office, swept the room for any possible trace of electronic surveillance devices, and killed power to all but the feeblest lighting.

"So," Monroc started, "not only did the council refuse to give you approval, they shut down your research?"

"That's right. They held an immediate vote, and before I even left the office had closed down the laboratory. They had the right, legally, to do it, and I am not surprised that they did. They're afraid – I can't blame them."

"If they get a hint about our second lab," Stapleton said, "they'll shut that down, too."

"Legally, they can't – it's a military operation," Monroc stated matter of factly.

"They could find a way, though," Forrester added. "The public would be just as fearful, just as outraged, just as passionate – and there'd be no chance of convincing them otherwise. I knew that going into the council chambers. I fully expect to be hit with a Hearing of Removal notice just for suggesting it. What I am here for right now is to make the final decision of what we must do."

"What you told the council," Monroc said, "is completely true. Without a solution to the Bryce Effect, we will lose, and within a couple months. We don't know what kind of attack they are amassing, but we believe it's big. We can't recover from it. We can't shoot them all down, and we can't cover every inch of ground. If they looked like Hybrids or Brodians maybe we could find a way to detect them from a distance. We just don't have the military strength. You know this – you have as much military background as I do."

"I do know it. I just needed to be sure. Doctor – tell me that we can do this, and that we won't be dooming the humanoid race to something worse than the Bryce."

The doctor sat silently for a moment. He chose his words carefully. "Mr. Forrester… I believe with everything that I know as a scientist, that we would be releasing a benign genetic mutation, barely noticeable within the human genome. I believe it. I am nonetheless scared, petrified, not only of what we simply don't know, but that you're asking me to make that decision."

"I'm not – the choice is mine. I just need your opinion. General Monroc says that without it we will lose, and probably all be dead within months. Is this better than certain death – and how quickly would it take effect?"

"It's better than certain death; I can say that absolutely. The effect would take a day at most. We can introduce the catalyst directly into the atmosphere of Concourse planets. It's smaller than nanotechnology, can be seeded in multiple locations, will self-replicate for a specific period of time, and will be carried throughout the planet in roughly a day. We have encoded it to stop self-replicating after that period of time. All it takes is your order. If we're going to do it, the sooner, the better. I don't think we had any leaks in our lab, but if they exist, we have hours, maybe minutes before we're discovered.

Forrester didn't hesitate. "Do it."

CHAPTER FOURTEEN
CONCOURSE HEADQUARTERS
15:22:25

Two events, practically, coincided: the reports of a Bryce attack which, despite exposures, resulted in no deaths, and the return of Dunn and Ser to Concourse space. Dunn remained in hospital; while the damage done to his body was halted by the transfusion for Ser, it was not reversed, and he would spend a while in recovery.

The reports of Bryce attacks continued, and it became suddenly clear that the Bryce Effect was halted. Forrester immediately released a statement that, while not revealing any details of the solution, announced that a permanent answer to the Bryce threat had been discovered and implemented. Questions surrounded his office, and both the War Committee and the Concourse Council were demanding information, but the overall reaction throughout the planets was relief and joy.

Proxima Ser was ushered into Forrester's office and he welcomed her warmly. She recounted as much of her ordeal as she could remember, and while it contained nothing that wasn't in her written report, Forrester listened intently.

"You should know," she added, "that I was approached by Merwa Yon, and he tried to convince me that I should report to him directly, to bypass you. I'm told he's no longer with your office, but I'm duty bound to report the contact nonetheless."

Forrester smiled softly. "I understand that your philosophies and mine differ in some respects, that perhaps yours are more closely aligned with Yon's

– nonetheless I am grateful that you chose to report to me."

"It wasn't really a choice – I'm a soldier, and we follow the orders we're given."

"Monroc would be pleased to hear that." Forrester had come to rely on the traditional, order-following, blindly obedient and yet full of criticism that came from Monroc – strange how those he differed with most – Monroc, Taylor, Zavis, and others – always seemed to be those he trusted and relied on.

"On that, Sir – I am aware that our mission violated some of your orders. While I wasn't dir---"

"Your orders were based on assumptions, Lieutenant – no more and no less than my decision to send you in the first place. This might not be very military in thinking, but there are times when orders are unimportant. Duty can often require the rejection of orders, to serve the greater good. Dunn chose to alter the mission, knowing full well that he faced serious consequences if he was wrong in doing so. He wasn't – he's a hero to the Concourse, as are you, and any alterations in the mission were necessary results of having more information than I did."

Relieved, but somewhat confused, Ser asked, "Then the end justifies the means?"

"Yes – if the ends are important enough, the means don't matter. You choose the best option from those available to you. My history includes what some would call unorthodox methods. The result is what matters."

Ser smiled – for the first time, Forrester thought, in the time he'd known her. "I've seen the reports – about the Bryce, I mean. The mission was a success, I guess, so I couldn't argue."

Forrester paused for a moment, then told her that he hadn't used her information to thwart the Bryce. Her observations, he explained, while it might have led to an answer, would have taken weeks, if not months to implement. Its effectiveness was uncertain, since she's only had the chance to test it on one person and not under any controlled conditions. In the meantime, they had an alternative which was certain of success, and immediately. Her mission, he said, was nonetheless a huge success, and contributed critical information about the Bryce. He explained, more than he had to any other person outside of Monroc and the medical staff, what led them to the discovery and how it worked.

Ser stared at the floor for a long while, during his explanation and after. "What about racial purity? Have you given any thought to the effects it will have on each planet's uniqueness?" Her tone admonished.

"At the time, the choice was between possibly compromising - theoretically only – some level of uniqueness between human planets, and risking their deaths. Without turning this into a discussion of whether planetary uniqueness – which is of doubtful value in my opinion, and may remain fully intact – is the issue, of the two options, this was the one which could give us what we needed more than anything else – immediate results."

Their conversation continued for a short time, but Forrester sensed that Ser had lost interest in hearing more. She argued that the chemical blocker had a strong chance for success, and that racial purity demanded it have the chance. Forrester couldn't see her point of view. To him, racial purity – or rather, racial and planetary differences, had plagued the Concourse from the days before it even existed, and had caused countless deaths through the conflicts it fostered and the solutions it prevented. To Forrester, any diminishing of racial purity was a blessing, a positive side effect of the solution chosen.

***

The Bryce attacks halted. Once it was obvious that the Bryce Effect was useless, the ships stopped coming. The planets of the Concourse erupted with joy – another enemy had been vanquished. Forrester was hailed as a hero, and as the story came out – first through rumor, then through official statements, the Concourse had more heroes: Henn Dunn, Proxima Ser, General Monroc, Doctor Stapleton and his staff, and a young farm boy from Idona, Caleb Alletson, who risked his life in an instant to prove that the Bryce Effect could be stopped. The concerns about the solution, of course, started – but in the celebrations of peace, something the Concourse enjoyed all too little of, those arguments were softly spoken and small in number. Only slowly did the ultimate problem start to emerge.

***

When Ser received the invitation to appear before the War Committee she welcomed it. Except for visiting Dunn – whom she disliked, and didn't respect his views or his actions, but nonetheless owed her life to – she stayed home. The Concourse had gone crazy. People celebrated victory that came at too great a cost, and hailed as heroes those who had done little more than betray their own people and aided in the betrayal of hers. She explained her discoveries, and didn't shy away from voicing her opinions once she understood she was in the company of like minds. The conversation – which took place in private – took a long time, and when done Merwa Yon asked to see her privately. She explained her reasoning for reporting to Forrester, and expressed regret. The result, Yon explained, would have been the same since Forrester had used illegal tactics and hid information from the Committee. Even had Yon known what Ser had to share, Forrester still would have beaten them to the punch. Forrester hid Ser's information, though, and acted without anyone's consent. He no longer deserved the loyalty she had by rights given him. The Concourse was poisoned. Ser agreed.

***

Political success was never something Forrester took for granted; it comes and goes quickly. The War Committee, though without legal authority, still had the support of the council, and in peacetime the council carried more power than the Director. The committee continued to attack Forrester and his office. The solution which Forrester rejected and kept secret, they claimed, would have worked, and without the extreme measures and possible disastrous effects of a DNA mutation.

"Did you have the Ser report in time to consider it?" Monroc asked.

"Yes. I received it a day before we released the mutation," Forrester replied. "I considered it, but we had no time. You said yourself that in a couple months the Bryce would have effectively destroyed the Concourse planets. We had the solution, and the chemical blocker could have taken months to put into place. It wasn't a viable option."

Monroc rubbed his hands over his face. "Is this something you put before Stapleton or the other medical staff? The chemists? Someone with greater knowledge about such things than you? You're a politician, a statesman, and you have a military background, but you're no scientist. Did you put this before anyone else, to confirm your conclusion that there was no time to give this a chance?"

No, Forrester said, he hadn't. Thousands died every day, millions could die in a week. Forrester himself had made the decision. Monroc shook his head – was this abuse of power, or brave use of it? He didn't know, but he wasn't comfortable with the state of things right now.

***

Where the first report came from no one could later say, but it was probably started locally, a news item of minor note, a curiosity item. Only when it was noticed in other places, over wider areas, did it become hard news, and before a couple days had passed it was all over the Concourse vid: since the mutation had been released no one had died at the hands of the Bryce, but there had been few new pregnancies. In a human population of trillions over almost three dozen planets, there had been only a handful of positive tests for conception. The non-human members of the Concourse continued to reproduce as always; the problem was confined to humans. While it was suggested that it could be a latent side effect of the Bryce, it was quickly pointed out that during the weeks of war there had been no sterility – only after the mutation had this happened. Immediately scientists went to work on finding a solution. The worlds considered the fact that the human race could disappear in a generation if they weren't successful. The War Committee – still in effect although war had long since ended, recommended to the council that they hold a Hearing of Removal of the Director, Charles Forrester. The vote to hold that hearing was unanimous.

***

The man the two people needed couldn't be found on Teretania. Instinctively they knew that to find an assassin, someone who could do the job and who would never betray their secrets, they had to venture outside the Concourse, to the infamous Blish Colonies.

Within the sphere of Concourse planets, but not allied with that government in any way, the Blish colonies were fourteen inhabited planets covering almost a hundred lightyears of space. The people of the Blish colonies rejected any form of central government. Even on the individual planets any attempt to organize into a strong government was fought – violently, and always successfully. It was always said that you could live, raise a family, be successful in business or art, do anything you wish in the Blish colonies as long as you didn't run up against someone stronger than you who didn't like you. Protection organizations existed, and municipalities (of a sort) serviced the needs of people – but always as a business, and never without profit. In this seemingly lawless frontier there was little war and less crime than in more civilized areas – but nonetheless if you wanted to find a criminal, this was the best place to look.

Proxima Ser carried two blasters, only one of which she displayed. She kept her hand in a natural pose, neither close to nor too far away from the weapon. Confidence mattered more than actual ability, at times – reputation and the assumption of skill would prevent more trouble than actual skill. Merwa Yon carried one blaster, and kept his hand close to it. He looked nervous, Ser thought – though perhaps less because he was entering a true den of murderers than because he might be recognized. So might she, although here of all places it was less likely, and here of all places it didn't matter.

Legends are interesting, she thought – and when they turn out to be true, all the more so. On the planet Good Will, in a small town well north of their arctic circle, was reported to exist a league of assassins. They never advertised, and they never confirmed their existence, but for a hundred years stories of their deeds traveled with the spaceships of the human worlds. Ser wondered if the stories were true, and as a younger woman Ser had imagined being assigned to infiltrate this league and bring it down, the heroic deeds of a Concourse secret agent. Now she walked directly into their lair (she could think of no less-cliché term, given the nature of their business), but as what? Was she a hero to the human people of the Concourse, or a traitor to them? To the Concourse government she felt no allegiance, no need for loyalty – they, starting with Forrester, had betrayed everything the Concourse was built for – protection of the human worlds. First they invited aliens into the Concourse, and now they had unleashed the disease that if it didn't cause the extinction of the human races, would certainly lead to the end of the humans as the dominant species in this part of the galaxy. Her loyalty was no longer to the oppressive and government of the Concourse – it was to the people who didn't know what had happened to them.

On this dry planet, despite the cold, very little snow fell. Tiny drifts less than a foot high gathered in the corners of the building, reflecting the bright orange sun but failing to raise the temperature above frostbite level. They wore clothing slightly out of style for the frontier, but they didn't seek to hide that they were outsiders; the Assassins League wouldn't perform their services in the Blish Colonies, one of their codes of honor. They stepped into the doorway of a stone-and-mortar building, shook off their coats, and stepped into the strangest sight Ser had ever seen.

The room wasn't large, but it was incredibly bright – and warm. The ceiling glowed with artificial yellow light common to most human planets. The walls sparkled with crystals that reflected and separated the light into many colors, a prismatic effect that gleamed off the surface of the pool which filled nearly half the room. The temperature was hotter than the equator on Ser's own planet. Naked women and men sat along the edge of the pool while others swan. Ser had seen many instances where people tried to bring the feel of outside indoors, but never with such skill – and such expense. She felt that she remained long her skin would tan – and judging by the skin-tone of the human women she saw, it wouldn't take very long at all.

Merwa Yon grunted disapproval at the sight. Ser neither approved nor disapproved – not caring, really, the life that others choose for themselves. Perhaps the women were hired companions, perhaps the men were, or maybe they were colleagues enjoying fun. What did it matter? She couldn't see herself taking part, but had no objections.

"You object?" she asked quietly.

"I do," he replied. "Where I come from we don't display ourselves publicly. Both the men and the women defile themselves in this way. Besides, we have more important matters."

From the other side of the room a man approached. He was fully clothed, although in light blue garments to match the tone of room.

"I am Falson Penn," he said, placing his hands together in a typical Alleghanian greeting, then reaching out his right arm as Earthers would expect. "I was told to expect you. Please, we should move to another room because you'll certainly become too warm in here, dressed for the outside as you are."

They followed him past the playful scene and through a heavy stone door. The cooler air hit them both and they sighed, refreshed to be out of the sweltering heat behind them.

The room was spartan, with a long table and four chairs, two on each side. The walls were bare but for one sign, written in Earther: THE LAW ABOVE ALL ELSE. Yon looked at the sign for perhaps a few seconds longer than he should. Penn appeared to be middle-aged, stood slightly taller than Yon, was not overly muscular, but presented a very relaxed and confident manner. His carried the long locks typical of his people, and a mustache of the same white-gray color. He motioned Yon and Ser toward two of the seats.

"Laws," Penn said, "are created by men. Every country, every planet, every organization, has its own laws, and they often differ in both intent and style. Our laws, Mr. Yon, are as important to us as yours are to you. We have codes, and violation of them brings punishment and shame. Adherence brings honor and satisfaction. Who's to say that one set of laws is better than another? Trust me, if your laws were enough, you wouldn't be here."

Yon looked at Penn. The assassin's perception was keen, because Yon had already concluded that laws were only good when the right people wrote them.

"Are you the assassin?" Yon started.

"No, but I am his leader. When dealing with someone from outside the League an assassin doesn't meet with the customer. That way there is no concern of a betrayal later on, because there has been no conspiracy to fear. Here –" he indicated the area with a sweep of his arms – "we are protected by the League and peace of lawlessness, but since all of our work must take place outside the Blish colonies, we have to take some precautions."

Yon was sour. "How do we know the task will be completed?"

Renn laughed. "Have you ever heard of a member of the League of Assassins failing to kill a victim – that's right, we don't bother to euphemize, we kill for money – without the failure himself being killed? Never."

"We didn't mean to insult you," Ser said. "This is a new realm for us."

"There's no insult, Ms. Ser. What we do is illegal in your world, and therefore misunderstood. However, we can only do it in your world, to protect our own, so we accept misconceptions. We're as reliable as the warranty on a private yacht-cruiser. Who is the victim?"

The conversation continued for a long time. The League of Assassins charged based on the importance of the victim, using their own formula, and this target required a stiff price. Finally an agreement was made, and a time frame decided. No papers were signed, no collateral needed – simply put, the kill would be made and then the payment received, or another kill would be made (two, in this case). There was no malice in the arrangement, no unfriendliness, and Ser walked away confident that their plan would move forward easily.

Yon walked away with the same feeling, only he had additional plans, plans that Ser would never know about until it was too late. She was a tool, a disposable tool.

CHAPTER FIFTEEN
TERETANIA – CONCOURSE HQ
15:23:19

The Bryce representatives surprised Forrester. He had expected, given the xenophobic character of the Bryce, that they would be shy, meek, and submissive. These men and women – four in all, were the opposite. They stood tall, confident, and spoke with authority. Their spokesman, who went by the name of Easternly (the closest approximation, he said, to typical Concourse pronunciation) showed none of the traits that many people anticipated. The negotiations went quickly, though the Bryce, even in defeat, were not willing to accept anything unconditionally.

"We demand that our borders be respected at all times," he said, his voice a deep bass that commanded attention.

Forrester spoke briefly with his three negotiators – two he picked and one the asked he council to provide – and replied, "It has never been our intention to cross your borders, except in friendship." To mention the Bryce incursions into Concourse space and the millions killed, though certainly justified, would be pointless. There was no argument over what happened, only why – and even the why at that point was second priority to insuring that it didn't happened again.

"We have looked over the cartographic boundaries you brought and suggested (he chose that over the word *demanded*, which the Bryce negotiators preferred to use), "and they are acceptable, subject to approval by our ruling council." The council would not be happy, because the boundaries included no increase of Concourse space, significant areas of the galaxy surrounding Bryce space which would be forbidden to Concourse traffic, and the terms included severe penalties for crossing those borders, whether intentional or not. Still, they would approve it. The Bryce still had secrets, communications and space flight abilities that were beyond Concourse technology, which they wouldn't share but which they would certainly use should war break out again. They were still to be feared to a degree, because a new Bryce Effect might be possible.

"Why is your ruling council not here?" said a young woman, a part of the Bryce contingent. She was dark-skinned, with deep black eyes and black hair that shined. She was incredibly beautiful, Forrester noted, but her voice, too, commanded respect independent of any beauty. "If we're to complete these discussions, the authority should be present. We act as authority for our race – can you not speak for yours?"

Her logic was unmistakable. Forrester could negotiate, but in truth he couldn't make a commitment that couldn't be overruled by the council. He didn't converse with the others – he knew what to say.

"Our ruling council is a large body – making negotiations unwieldy. They will meet immediately after our talks and you'll have a decision within a few hours. Before the day is out you can be on your way back to your people."

"We don't return to out people," she said. "Our role has always been to be the point of contact with contaminated people. We protect our race by giving ourselves over to contamination. We have the authority to enter into a treaty for our people; that's all that matters to you."

A new picture of the Bryce came to Forrester. Just as their warriors were trained, possibly from birth, to give themselves up in battle, never to return, so were their negotiators. The agents accepted their role, not knowing any other options, and perhaps they were designed in special ways for the task. Certainly these were the most imposing Bryce he had seen. He wondered: would they move into exile somewhere, be willing to join the Concourse people, or would they end their lives, believe their purpose to be done?

"The terms will be approved," Forrester said.

Another Bryce, a male with blonde hair, eyes which were a light blue that appeared white at times, and features which would be considered handsome in any race, said, "No race has ever taken such extreme measures to attack us." Forrester understood that he meant defend, but it is not conceivable that the Bryce would consider any action taken to be other than attack. To fight against the Bryce Effect, even on your own world, is an attack. It's how they are trained to think. "The race you call Gorups attacked through surrender and agreement. Those we called DeVaun attacked by fleeing. You reused to agree, you refused to flee. The terms must be firm while we protect ourselves during your slow elimination."

The negotiators of the Concourse stiffened. Forrester wasted no time. "Are you saying that your plan remains to eliminate us. If that's the case, there can be no truce, no treaty. We won't negotiate under threat of any kind.

"No, we need take no action to eliminate you now. Your method of attack has accomplished that task – you have eliminated yourselves."

***

The council approved the treaty with only a few dissenting votes from the non-human members. The human planets faced a greater issue, and the Bryce, if they could just be put aside for a while, could be dealt with later. There were few that didn't see the Bryce as a legitimate threat, and fewer still who didn't want some revenge against them, but for many people the new enemy, the architect of their troubles, was a man they hailed as a hero only days before – Charles Forrester. The Hearing of Removal would be the following day, and his removal was a certainty.

Merwa Yon resigned the War Committee – now call the Committee to Ensure Peace – because the committee refused to reproach the council for adopting the treaty and refused to demand the arrest of Forrester before he was removed from office. These steps, Yon said, would solidify the committee power for all time and keep the council in line. Forgetting momentarily that four members of the Committee were council members, he created a controversy that he didn't remain around to argue.

***

In his quarters Forrester and Alphan sat in silence for a while. No strategy would stop the inevitable result from the next day – he would be removed from office and quickly arrested. He had expected this result after the Battle of Teretania, and accepted that fate. When it didn't happen he was surprised, but knew that the day could come again, as it had.

"Do you regret it?" she asked, sitting on the sofa with him, her legs pulled up under her hips, their blue skin deep in the dim light of the room.

"I don't see how I can," he said. "I regret the result, though I still believe it is just a temporary problem. There are pregnancies in the Concourse, and these people have been shown to have adopted the mutation, so the sterility – or whatever the problem is – will be overcome. In the meantime, weeks or even months of fighting and dying have been stopped. It will cost me my job, my freedom, and maybe my life. Outside of the time I won't get to have with you, though, I can't regret it. Was I wrong?"

Of course you were wrong!" she said strongly. "You were wrong to send the Taylor when you did, you were wrong to send Dunn and Ser on their mission, and you were most wrong in hiding Ser's information from the council or the scientists. You were arrogant, impatient, obsessed, and thoroughly wrong."

He stared at her. A hundred arguments formed in his mind, but he held them back.

Her expression changed. "Maybe," she added.

The comm buzzed. In his quarters only a handful of people could reach him, so he had to answer. At the pother end the face of Garl Zavis looked back, his expression surprise. Or was it happiness? Confusion?

"Charles, you need to get over to my apartment right away."

"Garl," he said, "I'm spending the night with Alphan. We're not sure we'll have more."

"Trust me – you want to come."

That was enough. Within minutes Forrester and his lover were using a private transtube to reach Zavis' quarters outside the headquarters property. Given the weight of everything else, the sum of which Zavis was completely aware, this had to be some critical news to pull him away tonight. The trip took almost an hour, the Teretanian offices and Zavis' quarters far away from the Concourse property.

They talked along the way about unimportant matters. Their conversation about Forrester being wrong (maybe) could be picked up again later, should they decide to do it. They entered the Zavis' quarters. It was one of the most colorful Forrester had seen, with old-fashioned fixtures littered throughout – free-standing lamps, an old style vidscreen that originally had a cord attached to accept programming, and photographs printed on paper hanging on the walls. Canthay Zavis had not only accepted human tastes, she embraced it, ran with the idea and made it her own. The home-like nature of the apartment made the generic term "quarters" ridiculous.

"This is so amazing," Alphan said. "I mean, I don't understand a tenth of it, but it's just beautiful." Canthay started to show Alphan different pieces, and they moved throughout the home, eventually entering another room. Garl Zavis seemed to be waiting for that moment to speak. Forrester, despite his impatience, let him.

"I was going to call you here in the morning for something else, but couldn't wait. If you heard it somewhere else…I mean, I guess I wanted you to be the first."

"Garl – what's up? I've never seen you like this. I've seen you prepared to die and not half this anxious."

"The mutation isn't going to stop the human races from reproducing."

Forrester believed that all along. "I know. There's always an answer."

"No, you don't understand – the answer has been found. The pregnancies that have happened throughout the Concourse are almost all the result of inter-planetary mating. The mutation is preventing DNA strands that are too similar from reproducing, but those of different planets, or those few from the same planet which are different enough genetically, are able to conceive. It'll mean a completely new Concourse – one where planetary boundaries don't mean anything, but the Concourse will be sustained. I learned about it today through my own sources – I've picked up a few tricks from you along the way when it come to intelligence – but figured you were too embroiled to get much information outside your own political troubles."

Forrester hadn't heard anything, though of course news like this would be all over the vid quickly. The reaction would be hard to gauge. The Concourse would be saved, but the Concourse would never be the same. If indeed the only people who could freely conceive children were those who came from different planets, something which was difficult before due to DNA differences between them as much as the social problems, the challenges of unity were gone forever. Forrester smiled. He had fought for

173

unity through political means and through argument, and through the necessities of war, for more years than he could count. Now unity would be forced on everyone. He couldn't resist the sense that he had accomplished it, even though the effects of the mutation were something he could not have predicted. If he could have predicted it, not only would he have done the same thing, he would have done it with no resistance or concern at all.

"Garl, thank you for telling me – but why did you need us to come here? It's good to see you – we haven't seen much of each other in ages – but what's your ulterior motive?"

Forrester heard Alphan cry, "Oh my – you're not kidding!"

Garl Zavis smiled. "I guess you're not the first to know. Canthay is pregnant."

The two women reentered the room, both smiling. Forrester's jaw stood open. Finally he composed himself. "Wha – wait. But, Canthay's not even humanoid. Interplanetary is one thing, but ---"

"It's your mutation," Canthay said, her face bright and her long hair draped across her shoulders. "It hasn't just made interplanetary conception easier – well, compulsory – it has bridged the gap between other species. That little nanomutation has not only made it possible for other species to interbreed, it's given someone like me – someone who had no chance of reproducing, being an alien mule of sorts, the chance to reproduce."

"We don't know how this will go," Zavis added. "Any child of ours would be completely different. It contains Gorup DNA, Brodian DNA, some elements that are strictly designed by the

Hybrids, and my human DNA. It may not be viable in the long run, and we don't know what kind of life such a child would have. We don't know. But we're not going to turn down the chance to find out, or deny that creature a chance to live."

They talked for a while, still standing. The concept was amazing, Forrester decided. In his most wild imaginings, though he hoped planets of the Concourse would intermingle over time, and he looked for cooperation with all species and races throughout the galactic arm, the idea that all species could mate, could intermingle, might one day find their differences blurred and hidden in the mix of life in the galactic arm, never entered his mind. It wouldn't help in his current troubles, though. Most people wouldn't see the long view – they weren't capable of doing that. Hatred, prejudice, racism, these are passions much too strong to be argued away. There would be dark days ahead for the Concourse, because it would resist this solution for a long time before embracing it – but one day it would have to, because it had no choice. That would be long after he was vilified, long after his life was over, practically if not literally.

"...and that's why you have to go," Zavis continued. Forrester had been lost in thought, and hadn't comprehended his friend's words.

"What?"

"You need to go – resign, and disappear. I said I was going to call you over here in the morning – that's why."

"What do you mean? I can't just disappear. Look, I made the choices I made, and I'll face the consequences."

"Why?" Canthay said. "Who says you have to pay the price for doing what no one else had the guts to do? You're a hero in a lot of eyes, and years form now what all the dust settles from the events of the last – well, twenty years – you'll get the credit you deserve, but we all know that right now you are going to take a lot of blame. You deserve it, for some of your actions, but you don't deserve all of it, and on balance you did what anyone with your foresight would have done. Take Alphan, resign tonight and get out. We have a network in place to get you out."

Three pairs of eyes stared at him. Forrester turned to Zavis. "You've set up an escape for me? You know this isn't how I do things."

"How you do things? When have you ever done things twice the same way? You've spent your life doing your duty. Along the way you've broken every law and custom known to civilized man, and never once have you let legality or anyone else's perceptions guide you – you've been dictator and played God more than once. Along the way, though, you've save the human race a couple times. Even today, your actions were totally wrong by every convention we know – but one day it will be plain that it was the action which again saved the humanoid race. I believed this before Canthay and I got the news, so I'm not blinded by gratitude. You'll be convicted of crimes you had to commit by people who'll never be able to see that you did them a great service. You'll be imprisoned, maybe executed, maybe assassinated, I don't know. You don't deserve that. Frankly, neither does history, and you don't want the guilt of your death to haunt the future Concourse."

Forrester said, "Monroc and Stapleton, some of the others..."

"They have already been approached, and Stapleton is already far away from Teretania. Monroc will go if you do, but not otherwise. Anyone else who could face consequences they don't deserve is being ferried away. Frankly, you're the last to find out. Take Alphan, go find a life in the Blish Colonies. Go live somewhere on an island in the middle of an ocean. Look for Ian Taylor if you want – I know you've thought about it."

Forrester looked at Alphan. She had tears in her eyes, beautiful yellow tears that turned her skin a mellow green. "Alphan, I.....if you came, it would be difficult, at best."

She smirked. "Did you not hear? You're the last to know. I've known for days, and made the decision to come with you two minutes after I learned. Why do you think it was so easy to tell you how wrong I thought you were? I'd never do that if you faced what you'd have to face. I don't know if I share Garl's view of history, but even if I don't, my life has been with you for a long time. Who knows – maybe you've mutated us a child in there somewhere. It doesn't matter."

Once assured that Zavis was insulated from blame, Charles Forrester left Teretania. They didn't set foot back on the Concourse section of the ship – Zavis said it would be too dangerous, he might be subject to arrest. Forrester submitted his resignation from a ship piloted by Henn Dunn, who would be heading to Bryce space to secretly collect the non-xenophobic refugees he learned about during his mission. It was not a Concourse-sanctioned mission – it was his duty to other humans.

Forrester had been Director of the Concourse for over fifteen years. It had hard times ahead, and the leadership might not be up to the task. The council now controlled most of the government, and that isn't a situation he wanted to see. Suddenly, he realized, it didn't matter. He had done all he could. He had done his duty. He had been willing to die for that, but now it wasn't his duty anymore. His only duty was to live, and to Alphan. He reached over and caressed her blue hand.

**

Tebols prided himself on his detachment, his ability to perform his job without emotion. In nearly twenty years as an assassin, with almost seventy kills to his credit, he'd come to think of emotions as something for lesser men, for neophytes.

But his hands were shaking.

A month or two earlier it would have been impossible to enter Teretania. His lineage – or because of his lack of lineage – would have made him suspect. His planet, deep in the Blish colonies, kept no records, and in the panic and emotion-filled days of the Bryce war, travel to Concourse worlds was restricted. Today, however, he walked onto Teretania with only minimum identification (forged) and strode easily toward his target.

His hands still shook.

He walked the slidewalk toward the nearest hotel and settled in. For a few weeks he waited, visited shops and talked with people, creating a pattern of normalcy, a pattern of total insignificance, waiting for the day when he could strike. Once done, with a target of this magnitude, leaving would be difficult, and would take a very long time, so to ride out the storm that would follow and avoid suspicion he had to be careful. When he got home, he would be a legend.

Hopefully, before the day arrived, his hands would stop shaking.

***

Proxima Ser had been watching the newspapers and the vid for weeks, trying to determine when the opportunity would arrive for the assassin to strike. Public appearances were common enough, but she supposed that the assassin would pick an event that was not only public, but that was planned far enough in advance that he could devise a way to have a weapon in the area. Security would be tight everywhere Zavis and Chine traveled, and Teretanian security wouldn't allow any weapons nearby.

She had considered resigning her commission in the CDF shortly after the truth about the mutation was known. Now she had new plans, something that would reverberate throughout the human worlds. Cahill, the publisher, would be her mouthpiece. It would take months to get started, and more units than she had, but more than enough people agreed with her way of thinking. It would only take time, and time would bring money – money would secure Cahill.

But first she had to make sure one more death took place. She couldn't miss this; too much was at stake.

The admission ceremony for the Postilian Embassy had been known for weeks. The forty-ninth member of the Concourse would be yet another non-human member – the twelfth, almost a quarter of the Concourse. Learning of this had been all she needed to know. The world would change, and she had to make sure it changed the right way.

Her legendary status and notoriety gave her the ability to pick her assignments, so she asked for this – personal guard to Zavis and Chine during the ceremony. What better position to be in?

On the stage stood almost the whole of the Concourse Council – changed a lot in recent weeks, she thought, but still full of alien-loving blenders of humanity. Zavis, as President of Teretania, stood with them. Chine sat in the front row, a Hybrid among humans? Cahill and Yon explained their failure to expose her. Ser looked at the human figure with long blond hair – could Chine really be Hybrid? It seemed impossible, and when it was revealed that she was pregnant everyone, including Ser, knew that Yon and the others had to be wrong. The mutation had created some strange and horrible situations, but inter-species breeding was rare, and a Hybrid would be sterile by design.

The vid cameras hung from the ceiling or hovered nearby, leaving even the front rows for the more important dignitaries. The audience numbered in the hundreds of thousands in this massive auditorium – perhaps the only one of its kind in the universe. Everyone had been checked for weapons, so the size of the crowd didn't matter. One person or a million, unless someone wanted to walk up and take Chine by the throat in front of the crowd...but an assassin doesn't commit suicide. His plan is to kill Chine, and then escape – but from where? How? When?

Ser stood off to the side of the stage, keeping both Zavis and Chine is her line of sight, but not in view of the cameras or crowd. The CDF carried blasters, and she could have easily done the assassins job at any moment – but that would be suicide, and she didn't want that any more than the killer did. Explosives were always a concern, but Ser knew that this would never be the mark of an assassin – they would kill if needed, but not indiscriminately. That was bad for business.

One by one the top council members gave speeches. Experts predicted that within fifty years alien membership might match humans – just fifty years! The speeches she heard talked of this as inevitability, and as a good thing, though it was colored with secret fear. So many politicians, it seemed, now secretly embraced blending the planetary DNA because they saw it was the only way to maintain human superiority. Human dominance was essential, but not by diluting the purity of the races. She would show them a new way – the right way. It would take time.

***

For nearly three days Tebols had been in position. He'd slipped into the tiny electronics cabinet in the crawlspace just before the security teams sealed off access. He'd lived on the small rations he brought and lived with his own stench, because that's what was needed to get the kill done. Had he been discovered it would have meant first arrest, then prison, and then death, because the League would not allow failure. So he sat, soundlessly, waiting for the moment. He would never see his victim; he had memorized where she would be sitting – and hopefully no one would ever see him once it was done. He had just a few dozen meters to move to get into position. His status as legend was almost assured.

***

Ser scanned the room. Two guards stood inside each doorway, and there were two more outside each door. The walls were double-bulkhead alloy, with no windows. The stage was sealed. Along the walls, high up, on a balcony overlooking the room were dozens of Teretania Police and Concourse Defense Force troops. The assassin couldn't get past them even if he could reach that level.

A movement caught her eye. The tiniest shaking of a thin wire seemed to occur, but she wasn't sure. Ignoring the events around her, completely unaware of anything but her instinct, she watched.

One of the vid cameras hanging form the ceiling moved slightly. There was no wind, no breeze that high in the room, and even if there had been, only one of the hundreds of suspended cameras moved.

Then another, ever so slightly. Ser stared, knowing that a third certain movement would be needed to confirm her suspicions. She was still, unwilling and afraid to move at all lest she miss it.

There it was! A third camera shuddered so slightly that had she not been looking right at it she would have missed it completely. The third movement completed a line, a slow moving line that in just seconds would be directly over the spot where Canthay Chine sat. She took a breath.

Without a sound her blaster came out of her holster, moved in a lightning fast arc toward the ceiling, and fired. A red beam appeared and struck the ceiling. Three things happened: The ceiling erupted in a fiery glow as the coherent light shattered cameras and wires; the auditorium erupted in screams as people dove for cover, both from the blaster fire and the falling debris; a second later a human figure fell through the melted ceiling, a high-powered needle-rifllaser strapped to his body.

When she landed on the Bryce world Moogh, before Ser was captured she saw how widespread they were: The Bryce had taken over large section of the galaxy, larger than the Concourse, and no one had known. The aliens and other enemies were running rampant. When she learned of the Postilian admission, Ser realized that Canthay Chine was not the problem. Hybrid or not (and Ser didn't believe she could be), her death wouldn't stop the trend of racial mixing which was taking place and would take place for decades to come. Chine's death – and her subsequent exposure if she had been a Hybrid - would merely increase the fear that humans would ultimately be overrun by other species. It would merely increase the support for mixing planetary DNA. She agreed with Yon's philosophy of independent pure planetary races allied to maintain the supremacy of humans, but his methods were illogical. His hatred of Zavis, Chine, Forrester, and those who denied him the power he craved, far overruled any concern he had for the purity of humanity. She suspected he was insane. She couldn't cancel the assassination; such things were not allowed by the League. She couldn't reveal the plot to Zavis or Chine or to the council without implicating herself in the conspiracy. She could only do one thing – watch for it, try to stop it, and use the notoriety to advance her plans.

As Chine walked away from the scene with only a few bruises from falling debris, and Ser acknowledged the congratulations of those who slowly realized what she had done, she thought her plans had started well. She knew, however, that she had one more problem, a dangerous situation, one which she wasn't experienced in handling, one which might bring her life to a quick end.

CHAPTER SIXTEEN
TERETANIA
16:02:01

The Concourse had been peaceful for months. Forrester had disappeared, and while there had been rumblings and arguments that he should be charged and hunted, no charges were filed. It couldn't be determined if any laws had been broken. Some took his resignation as enough; others wondered if maybe he was a hero after all. In the end, the more pressing matters took over.

Scientists still looked for a cure to the mutation, but reports said that it probably wasn't coming, at least not any time soon. The Concourse, the human races specifically, if it was going to survive, had to promote interplanetary mating. The resistance was strong, even militant. Travel between planets was encouraged, and the restrictions all but eliminated. Although it would take years, and there would certainly be a period of low birth coming that would affect future generations, there started a slow homogenization of the humanoid planets.

The attack came without warning. That these were Bryce ships was unmistakable by the design, but these came firing weapons, equal in strength to a comparable fighter of the Concourse. The total number of Bryce ships engaged in the recent war against the Concourse numbered in the hundreds of thousands, but that was dwarfed by the fleet which swarmed around one large ship. The attackers numbered in the millions. Their blasts couldn't penetrate the hull singularly, but they coordinated their firing together in groups of ten, twenty and a hundred. They targeted specific places on the ship, critical areas of communication, of surface-based weapons, and where the Concourse fighters were housed. The alarm went out to all Concourse ships and bases, but most were hours or days away.

Garl Zavis stood at the Command Center. He controlled the Concourse fleet house in Teretania – a part of the new order of government. As orders were barked and soldiers moved quickly to gather information, Zavis stood almost silently while he assessed the situation.

"Release the fighters – all squadrons."

In the Battle of Teretania the ship had been unable to get the fighters out of their bays because the exits were too narrow and could be blocked – a necessity of those fleets being constructed secretly. Since then, however, they had learned and now the fighter bays were larger, and protected with greater weaponry. They would be outnumbered, but the fighters would get out.

"How long before reinforcements arrive?"

A technician looked up from his screen. "Communications have to be rerouted to secondary systems to get confirmation, but it looks like fifteen hours before the first will arrive."

"Damn! Something's not making sense – something's illogical about this." Zavis turned to Danal-Tern, his second-in-command of the fleet. Danal was a CDF officer, not a Teretanian, and was liaison between the fleet and the Concourse government at Teretania. "Danal, how did the Bryce know we would be stuck here, our engines undergoing maintenance, right here, right now? How did they show up, with bases more than fifteen hours away, carrying weapons they've never used before, which look very much like the blast of Concourse fighter blasters?"

Danal didn't have an answer and Zavis didn't wait for one. He moved across the room. "I need better outside communications – I went to talk with the Concourse Commander!" Johnson, the man in charge of the Concourse military – there was no office of Director at the moment – moved with the bulk of the Concourse fleet, which consisted primarily of border patrols.

Instantly everyone was thrown in the air; the floor seemed to simply drop from beneath them faster than gravity could pull them after it. Zavis hit with force, stumbled, and fell against the bulkhead. Everything shook violently. Garl Zavis knew the ship as well as anyone, even most of the engineers. This was something new – and something terribly bad.

"Get me a report! What's happening?" On the screens in front of him he saw multiple views of the battle. Concourse and Teretanian fighters, vastly outnumbered, battled Bryce ships. Bryce blasts attempted to destroy communication nodules, but ship-based cannons held them off, for the moment. The soldiers in space and on the ship were doing their jobs well. Zavis, once he took command of the Teretanian fleet (with much protesting from some council members) had kept them battle ready, kept them on watch all the time, particularly when stationary. It wasn't the Bryce, specifically, he feared, but they were only one of many possible enemies who could target the ship. Teretania, no longer Concourse headquarters, was still the most powerful vessel, and therefore the first and most likely target, as was proven here.

One screen showed Bryce fighters attacking a transparent dome. "Oh, no," Zavis said. With the ship parked in space families had moved outside the ship to enjoy something Teretanians seldom were able to – a surface. Now, Zavis watched as the dome cracked and shattered into a million pieces under the concentrated fire of hundreds of Bryce ships. The dome dissipated, and Zavis watched with others as hundreds – many thousands – of bodies floated up from the surface of Teretania.

It was easily the worst thing he had ever seen. The vantage point was distant, so he could only see the tiny figures float away. They were men, women, and children, he knew, though he could see no details from this viewpoint. He didn't want to.

Danal placed a hand on his shoulder. "I've got something else – something worse." Zavis was about to ask what could have been worse than what he'd just witnessed, but when he followed Danal's finger to another viewscreen that stretched high and wide above them, he understood. Their primary gravidrive engine had exploded, and gigantic sections of it, pieces miles long floated into space. That had been the force which moved the ship – the only kind of force which could have.

"Danal – that exploded from inside." He indicated how the blast emanated from deep inside, blowing out sections which were too far below the surface to have been affected by small fighters, no matter how many, and the fact that there was no fighter power concentrated on or around that part of the ship. In fact, they had purposely stayed away from it. "They knew it would blow."

Danal said quickly, "We've been infiltrated."

"We've been invaded!"

***

The Concourse bases finally arrived, and the tide of battle outside the ship had turned. Most of the Concourse fighters who had bravely left the ship hours earlier had been destroyed, but they had weakened the Bryce fleet, and when reinforcements arrived the Concourse ships, freshly fueled and ready, in a matter of hours eliminated the outside Bryce threat.

Inside it had just begun. The Bryce had infiltrated large sectors of Teretania. Almost a quarter of the ship was occupied by Bryce, and thousands of Teretanians had been killed. Teretania had seemed the one impenetrable place in the Concourse, but now she was just another boarded vessel trying to hold off invaders, invaders who didn't worry about getting home, who never planned on getting home, who stayed alive for no other purpose than to destroy the enemy.

In the Command Center Zavis held a conference of his generals and internal security forces.

"We need to evacuate the ship," said general Honter of Izar. "Take them to the bases. The outside threat is gone, now. We can't risk Teretanians unnecessarily."

"We can't spare the resources," Zavis said. "To evacuate the population would take us away from the battles raging now. We would give up too much ground if we do that. Move them back, yes – but don't spend time and effort to move them off the ship."

"What if the Bryce decide to destroy the ship? They control enough that they could do it."

One of the internal engineers answered. "No, they don't. Teretania's modular design precludes being able to expose more than a few square miles of ship to space at any one time, and the strength of her hull will resist their hand weapons. Except for sabotaging the primary gravidrive engine, they've shown no use of anything but hand-based weaponry. It's the same design which prevents them from cutting off our life support, or us from shutting off theirs. Decentralized controls."

The battle had gone on for days already. That it has been an inside job – that Bryce spies had infiltrated and somehow opened the doors, so to speak, for thousands of Bryce soldiers, was certain.

"How many men do we have in battle, and waiting?"

Danal read the numbers. "As of this morning we have 230,000 fighting right now in eleven primary sections. Another 102,000 are supporting and preparing. That's not counting wounded. The bases outside have spared all they can. They are afraid of attack from space again, so they won't contribute more men than they've already sent."

Zavis said, "This is the Bryce's last stand. If they had more they would have sent more. They don't want to destroy the ship – they want to take it. Like in the past, the value of Teretania, what makes her most difficult to defeat is what makes her the prize so badly wanted. The Bryce didn't have enough people and ships left to take on the whole Concourse, but obviously their treaty didn't mean anything. We should have seen – it made us more of a threat than ever in their eyes. They had one option – take Teretania, the most powerful ship in the Concourse, so it couldn't be used against them, and if possible, use it against the rest of the Concourse. It's a flawed plan, because in the end they are trying to take a weakened Teretania that they couldn't use – and couldn't conceive that we never had designs on attacking them anyway. But flawed or not, they have a quarter of our ship and take a little more every day."

Zavis closed his eyes for a minute, and said so low that no one else likely heard. "Charles, I understand now."

He turned to his generals. "Unless you have a better idea than what we're doing right now, there's no other choice. The bases can't help us. What's on the way from other Concourse fleets and worlds won't be here for a while, and by then Teretania will be lost. We aren't winning and this isn't a stalemate – we're losing, slowly, but we're losing. Take everyone too young, too old, too sick or too scared, and cram them into the old Concourse headquarters sections, and seal it off from the rest of us until we can spare the manpower to move them to the bases. Take all the support troops – all of them, all 102,000, and get them in the battle. Go to the Teretanian population, and get more people. Anyone who is old enough to handle a gun and knows what to do with it, needs to be given one. Take every hand blaster off those bases if you need to – if they won't give them, have their commanders contact me, but we need to have them. The Bryce look like us, so make sure everyone who goes into battle, if not already wearing a CDF

191

uniform, has one. Make them – draw them on if you have to. I don't want anyone killed because he was confused with a Bryce. You find every young man, every young woman, and every person on this ship who can walk and has heard the name Caleb Alletson, and you get them into the battle! We're going to push the Bryce back and out of the airlocks today, or tomorrow there won't be any of us left!"

***

Gerje Greln had heard of Caleb Alletson, of course. He'd heard stories from his father about Garl Zavis and the time he uncovered the Hybrid threat in the middle of the Teretanian Senate chambers – with Gerje's father at his side. He had waited for the day he could join the Teretanian Police, follow in his father's footsteps. He'd read about Caleb Alletson and the Concourse – heck, he'd done his senior thesis on Caleb's farm life and his decision to join the Advance Patrol. When the Bryce attacked the ship he begged to be allowed to join the CDF, even though he wasn't old enough, but his father refused to let him.

Now he stood side-by-side with Concourse Defense Forces, Teretanian Police, and other civilians just like him. He held a blaster in his hand, and though he'd only been given an hour to practice, felt he knew what to do. He was given a uniform, though slightly too big, and he had been given a mission. It was the same mission everyone had – move forward, and anyone with a blaster in his hands that doesn't wear a CDF or Teretanian uniform is to be shot. He'd never killed anyone, but in the last few days had seen more death at the hands of the Bryce than he expected to see, ever. Killing them would be no problem. They planned to die anyway, he had been told, so even if you had a moral objection to it, you weren't depriving them of anything but the chance to take over Teretania and kill everyone.

Last week he was a kid, worried about whether he should ask Marianne Tepsa out on a date. Today, he didn't even know who that kid was.

The sergeant gave the order – move forward. He heard sounds of blaster fire up ahead, saw flashes down the corridor. He took his blaster off safety lock and moved forward.

CHAPTER SEVENTEEN
SOMEWHERE IN THE BLISH COLONIES

The first reports told of the siege of Teretania. The ship was under attack and had been boarded. Abandoned by the Concourse, it was sure to fall within days. Forrester didn't believe these reports. Certainly the Bryce had attacked, and it was a serious matter, but Teretania wouldn't fall quickly. Zavis was in charge, and he had too many skills, too much talent and intelligence, to let that happen – quickly, anyway.

The reports were sporadic and difficult to believe, but eventually the reliable vid and news-tubes made their way out to the frontier. The truth had turned out more incredible than any of the tales and legends could be. Over 400,000 men and women took place in the counter-attack to drive the Bryce from the ship – almost a quarter of those were civilians. *That* he could easily believe – if there were resources that could be used, Teretania and her leaders knew how to use them, and Teretanians would defend their ship to the death.

Forrester read a fictionalized account of a critical moment in the battle. He knew the dialogue was false, the events sensationalized, but he could see the events in his mind. He traveled there, like a fly on the wall; he watched what happened:

The young boy, not more than a teen, rounded the corner. Already in his short life he had killed a hundred Bryce, and been forced to walk over the bodies of just as many comrades. The Bryce and the human traitors made their last stand, but this young

Teretanian, followed (he hoped) by what remained of the Concourse Defense Force, would not be stopped.

Gerje Greln hesitated when he saw the uniform. In front of him stood Merwa Yon, once leader of the all-powerful War Committee.

"Soldier, what's your division?" Yon hollered.

Greln had no division; he wasn't even a soldier. His mind raced. The room, just six feet long and wide, was a litter of bodies, some Bryce, mostly human. He'd been told that the uniform was his only true way to tell friend from foe, and he knew this man, but something in his mind, some instinct he couldn't describe, told him not to relax. Perhaps it was his lineage (his father, Mike Greln, was part of Garl Zavis' task force to bring down the Hybrids years before), perhaps it was the mere hours of battle he had endured, but he remained at the ready.

"I have no division," he stammered.

The enemy understood that he faced a civilian, and chose that moment to strike. No weapon in his hand, he grabbed a pipe sitting inches away and swung it viciously toward the boy. Greln parried the blow with his arm, and could feel the bone crack as he was thrown backwards.

"What are you doing?" he yelled. "Have you allied yourself with the evil Bryce?"

"The Bryce understand," Yon hollered back as he tried to wrest the gun from the soldier's hands. "Planetary purity is the goal. The Bryce, evil though they may be, rebuke the species-mixing and genetic-mutating policies of Forrester and his cronies!"

The two, man and boy, fought to control the weapon. Greln said, "We're human – we're your people, and you have turned your back on us. You have soiled your honor with the bodies of your former comrades and turned traitor to the principles which you once held as a leader in the Concourse!"

The man laughed, a laugh so cold that it drove deep into the bones of the lad. "There'll be no humans before long. The Bryce offer a quicker death than the sterility and disfigurement that will come as the curse of Forrester's Folly takes hold throughout the Concourse. My thirty pieces of silver will be all I need, when the galaxy has been rid of the alien-loving people of the Concourse!"

"You're wrong, evil one! The Concourse is a good and peaceful place. We reject your prejudice and your betrayal."

Greln brought his foot up into the midsection of the older man, and he stumbled backwards, but the gun slipped from the boy's fingers. For a moment both looked at the instrument of destruction as it seemed to hold, suspended in mid air, as if it dared either of them to reach for it. Suddenly they both lunged. The weapon was grabbed, turned, and fired. One more body joined the ranks of the dead.

As more soldiers ran into the room, flush with the thrill of a victory, they saw a young boy, freshly stolen away from his quiet world, standing with his foot over the chest of a dead traitor, looking up as though at the stars above, thinking not of his heroism, but of the sweet girl back home who he hoped would understand that he did what he had to do – for her, for Teretania, for the Concourse, and for humanity in its many diverse, nearly infinite forms. That he had joined the ranks of Concourse heroes – entering the land of legend with Charles Forrester, Ian Taylor,

Garl Zavis, Caleb Alletson, and countless others, never entered his mind.

Well, perhaps for a moment it did, as he smiled.

How much, Forrester wondered, was true? That Merwa Yon was the traitor, that it was his power and mechanizations which allowed the Bryce to enter Teretania and begin their last, desperate attempt to eradicate humanity somehow – he was sure that was true. The evidence he saw supported that. Probably the young Greln had killed Yon – that seemed plausible enough. The rest was pure fiction, designed to make boys think of war in romantic and desirable terms, to fill their heads with glory and honor, to make killing something to invite, and death something to accept.

He turned his attention back to hard news, learning that the Bryce had been driven from Teretania, with great difficulty and terrible loss of life. Teretania itself was severely damaged. Zavis was elevated to legend status, and the talk was that the office of Director would be restored, with Zavis in that seat. The War Committee was disbanded, and government restructured. The Concourse lay in ruins, but rebuildable ruins. The mutation continued to restrict reproduction to interplanetary mates, or – with less frequency – inter-species mates. This had created a strange world, where men and women had to ignore centuries of racism and prejudice against everything different, just to survive. Here in the Blish Colonies, where government was rejected and where everyone was from somewhere else, this seemed easy to accept.

On Earth, on Izar, on Renna – it would be very difficult.

The news also spoke of pilot Henn Dunn, who had just returned from Bryce space where he rescued the non-violent Bryce refugees, including the old Bryce who had helped him rescue Proxima Ser. It was called a noble effort - but how, Forrester wondered, would these Bryce be received?

Proxima Ser also grabbed a few headlines. Since she saved Canthay Chine from an assassin's bullet at the Postilian ceremony she had become spokesperson for the newly-formed League of Planetary Purity. Their aim was to discourage interplanetary breeding, despite the dangers of a depleted population, and if the polls were correct the idea had a lot of support from the people of Concourse planets. If the condition remained stable, though, he expected that support would wane. People would understand the need to open social boundaries, perhaps reluctantly at first, but it would happen – it had to. Unless the survival instinct had been bred out of man somewhere along the way, it would have to.

He wondered what the connection was, if any, between Ser's heroism and the rumors running through the Blish colonies that she'd run afoul of the mythical Assassins League.

One last item caught his eye: a transcript of Garl Zavis' latest speech, where he outlined the rebuilding of the Concourse infrastructure, of Teretania itself, and how they would be dealing with the remaining Bryce. The tail end of the speech brought a small tear to his eye.

"Just as in the last war, and the war before that, it was Charles Forrester who led us to peace. I have been given credit for the final victory – although it was the people of Teretania who made the difference – but it was Forrester who saw the dangers before anyone else, who did his duty when he knew that many would hate and hunt him for it. Most people are starting to realize that the traitors who almost defeated us did so by first removing our most heroic leader. Had he been here, if we as a people hadn't been fooled, and if we hadn't been so short-sighted, the terrible events of recent weeks might never have happened. Mr. Forrester – we invite you back, to take your place in our world as you'll always have a place in our hearts."

It was a nice sentiment, although Forrester doubted that most humanoids would be ready to forgive his arrogance and his actions. Alphan said he was wrong. She may have been right. Or Forrester may have been completely right. Still, looking back, he couldn't see where his actions could be any but what they were. Should he return to the Concourse and help in the rebuilding? Zavis was more than capable, and Forrester, for the first time in his life, felt he'd done enough.

Instead, he looked over to Alphan, who caressed a tiny, blue-skinned baby boy. His life on this small planetoid of the Blish Colonies was simple, perhaps extra-legal in the traditional sense, and not always safe. But it was a life he could live, something he'd never done before. He decided to stay.

THE END

200

CONEY ISLAND CIRCA 4001

From *The Spacejacker Trial* by Richard Buchko

"Over there! I want to go over there!"

The seven-year-old's grip tightened and pulled the man along. His father's feigned resistance only made the effort more enjoyable. Hol Granthem looked up and the square building of metal with the grinning clown and the bleeding goat perched on top.

"Why do you want to go there to eat, Danal? There are so many places to choose from."

The boy never slowed down. "Teacher said that in the olden times people ate animals in places like that. I want to see what it is like -- can we, Dad?"

Already tired from their long day at the amusement park, Hol knew that arguing about dinner would just consume more energy. Besides, he'd always wondered what the ancient primitives really ate. This could be fun.

"Okay, we'll go," he said, "but after that we have to go home. Your mother will be waiting for us, and we have to get to bed early before our flight back to Mars in the morning."

The structure bore the most comical rectangular shape; an inefficient design, but then again, it was supposed to simulate the Ancient ways. Metal and stone walls - *who'd ever heard of such a thing?* - gleamed white under the light of the dome. The sculptures that surrounded the building didn't offer an appealing sight, but if you wanted authenticity, you had to sacrifice some common decency, especially when dealing with the Ancients.

They entered the building, and were greeted by a young woman in the same grinning clown costume. "Welcome to the Slaughterhouse!" she said with a huge smile. "Is your son over five years old?"

"I'm seven!" he said proudly, stretching his small frame to look even taller.

She bent down and placed something into his hands. "That's good. We don't allow the really young kids in here, because some of the practices of the Ancients were a little rough."

Hol was concerned. "We're not going to see any of the rituals, will we? I mean, roadkills or touchdowns, or anything like that? We just wondered what the food was like."

"Don't worry," she said. "We wouldn't resort to such things. No one really wants to see stuff like that. But the food items are interesting, and even if they don't taste exactly like the Ancients ate, we're proud of the presentation."

She explained the restaurant and showed them to a table with a plastic cover of red and white squares. Of course, modern restaurants would never have something so bold, but Hol remembered reading that the red was used to mask the blood marks on the table. How strange that the Ancients would make such a celebration of killing and ingesting animals, then try to cover the spots. Then again, much of what the Ancients did was confusing.

Hol turned to his son. "What did she give you, Danal?"

The boy opened his hand, and in it were four gleaming metal disks of various sizes. Each had the portrait of an Ancient king on one side, and on the reverse was the mutilated corpse of an animal lying under a pair of arches. These, the hostess had explained, were called money, and were part of the custom known as tipping, or getting screwed. The more you liked the meal, the more of these disks you left for the servers. In the days of the Ancients, at the end of the night the server with the most disks was rewarded, and ate the remains of the server with the fewest disks. It was barbaric, but Hol imagined it ensured good service at all times! Their server, who pretended to be very focused on the disks, winked at Hol and gave them each a thin sheet of paper that showed all of the items available. Hol was most interested in something that simulated the goat on the roof -- beef, it was called. So, he ordered a "beefurger." Danal chose a long gray meat nestled inside a piece of bread, called a "hot dog." Hol smiled, and wondered if young Danal realized that "hot dog" is what the Ancient pets were called also. It was customary to follow your ordering by saying "with fries and a coke"-- a blessing of some kind, he imagined. After a while their food came, and they began to eat.

The pictures along the wall fascinated the youngster. Hol explained that the Ancients had ancestors and deities who they called on in times of great crises or anger; they were called the Oh My Lords. It was hard to explain Ancient religion to such a young boy, but Danal was very smart, and wanted to learn. As Hol enjoyed his beefurger (which tasted very much like his typical wheat casserole) he did his best to teach.

"Danal, as you know, the Ancient Latins were considered the best scientists; the Ancient Africans were the best artists; and the Ancient Anglicans the adventurers. Each Ancient race specialized in some specific skill or science; because of that they surpassed us in many ways, although they were, of course, exceedingly cruel. The Americans, for example, were amazing politicians, but were also cannibals, known for inviting refugees from all over the world only to throw them into a huge melting pot. The Ancients believed that they knew everything there was to know; but sometimes, when they faced real trouble or wanted to conquer one another, they would call on their Gods. That one" -- he indicated a rather fearsome looking creature attacking a village in a colorful but violent painting -- "Was known as God Damn. His Latin name was Damnation, of course. He was the God of anger and rage."

"How about this one, Dad?" The boy indicated the painting directly above their table. A tall bearded man (truly an Ancient, to still have hair!) looked lovingly on a crowd of unhappy people, who had their hands outstretched as if waiting for something.

"Oh, him. You'll learn a lot about that one in school. He's the God of Questions and Uncertainty. He was called Geez; his ancient Latin name was Geezes. Whenever the Ancients felt they were treated unfairly, they would call to him to find out why. They would say 'Geez, why does this have to happen to me?' or 'Geezes, can't I ever get a break?'"

"Did he answer them, Dad?" A sharp young boy, Hol thought, to ask such questions.

"Well, of course the Ancients believed that he did, though we know in our enlightened day that it was just myth."

"Why did they believe he answered them, or how would they know?"

"The Ancients were very easy people to please. If they got what they wanted - for example if their enemies died or if they received a lot of these disks - they were said to have a prayer, which meant a good day. And they thanked a God. If it didn't happen, they never blamed Geez or the other Gods, because they believed that they must not have worked hard enough since 'the Gods help those who help themselves.' In those cases they accepted that they didn't have a prayer, and they still thanked God."

"The Ancients were funny people, Dad."

"Yes, they sure were, Son. It's good to know that 2000 years from now people won't be able to look back on our time and make fun of it. Now hurry up and eat your dinner."

"Hey, Dad! How about if we don't leave any disks for the server tonight? Maybe he'll say 'Geezes, why does this have to happen to me?'"

Hol smiled. His son showed great curiosity and intuition. Surely one day Danal would become a scholar, and although the truth about the Ancients had long ago been revealed, he would enjoy passing that story on to future generations.

END

SIT BACK AND ENJOY THE RIDE

An Earthman must defend himself in an alien trial, accused of the worst crime imaginable – you'll be shocked to find out what he did; five people set out in an experimental spaceship, not knowing that one of them has plans to take that ship where no one could imagine, and from where no one can return; a scientist discovers a way to correct every mistake you ever made, and he's willing to share that secret with you – for a price.

Take a few short trips through the universe – and maybe outside it.

THE SPACEJACKER TRIAL
AND OTHER SCIENCE-FICTION STORIES
by Richard Buchko

$9.99 - Shipped Free
Richard Buchko
Calumet History and Hobby
21671 Massie Road
Chassell MI 49916
906-369-0793
historyandhobby@yahoo.com

ALSO AVAILABLE AT AMAZON.COM
THE WORLD'S #1 BOOKSTORE

208

209

210

Made in the USA